With best regards
and thanks!

Augustus Doll

2023

TRIPTYCH

TRIPTYCH

David Augustus Ball

Triptych
©2018 David Augustus Ball
ISBN-13: 978-1-945979-01-9
v.1.3
This edition first published in Great Britain by Andalus
Publishing in 2017.
The right of David Augustus Ball to be identified as the author
of this work has been asserted in accordance with Section 77
of the Copyright, Designs and Patents Act 1988.

CONTENTS

FOREWORD

FOREWORD

My maternal grandparents—the only ones I ever knew—
lived beside and atop one another as husband and wife
for forty-eight years, until the freezing cold day in March
1997 when she, Lena, succumbed to liver cancer. In those
forty-eight years, I reckon that they had had about eight
minutes of what you hear television psychologists label
"marital bliss." This doesn't mean, and shouldn't be interpreted as evidence to prove, that they didn't love one
another. But, as a first-generation American, I knew better than most that affection had a more subtle meaning, at
least for those who met during World War II. My grandparents' love, like so many others', nourished itself, tested
itself, corrected itself, propelled itself forward on undercurrents of conflict and the spoils of an endless litany of
turf battles of one sort or another. Sometimes, it seemed
to me, as the silent witness, that there was no other con-
ceivable way for a couple to cohabit except in a state of
unarmed combat.

One of the fondest memories I have of my grandparents is nestled within those eight minutes: a road-trip to Lancaster, Pennsylvania that they took me and my brother on one late summer morning in 1971. My brother had seen pictures in some magazine of the Amish and their broad-brimmed black hats, horse buggies and scraggly beards, and it being terribly humid in New York on one of the few Saturdays that my grandfather didn't have to work over-time at the Boar's Head factory in Bedford-Stuyvesant, we—meaning they, my grandparents—decided to go on a road trip.

As if it were that simple.

That is the official memory, the one that my grandparents preserved in our family's oral recollection of family lore. The truth is that nothing in my grandparents' vocabulary could express or even grasp the concept of spontaneity. In fact, my grandmother never once, in all the years I knew her, went shopping for groceries at any time except Thursday mornings at 9:20. Therefore, whether the weather had been gorgeously mild on that particular Saturday in the summer of 1971, or it had started pouring rain, or even if New York suddenly, by some queer act of God, had been hit by a midsummer snowfall, was immaterial; we had been slated to take off for Lancaster at 6:30 a.m. for several weeks, and take off we would, come Hell or high water.

My grandfather, ever the planner, and not leaving anything to chance so as to forestall an eruption of my grandmother's wrath, drove one day to the corner of Kings Highway and Utica Avenue. There, head held high, his summer hat perched above his wrinkled brow, he entered the precinct of the American Automobile Association—the good old Triple A—of which he had been a loyal dues-paying member since the early 1960s, to get a Trip-Tik that would show him how to get from Avenue K in Canarsie to the fulcrum of Amish life in Lancaster. This little booklet amazed me then, and it amazes me even more now as it was the product of the pre-Internet era. This TripTik—and that is how the word was spelled out on the cover— was assembled by hand just for my grandfather by a stumpy man with a toupee who smelled of turpentine. Stumpy went over to a bookshelf, snatching the crotch of his polyester slacks out of the crack of his behind as he grabbed various little folded pieces of paper. He murmured out loud as if to convince us that he was doing something of the utmost importance in a code for which he was the lone breaker: "Let's see...21, 36N, 14, 17E...oh wait, no, that's not right...17W and...hmmm....where is it....yes, yes, 68." With this handful of little folded leaflets sloppily stacked in front of him, he wiped the sweat off his brow with a filthy handkerchief that he pulled from his desk drawer and started stamping little green arrows all over the maps to indicate the direction in which the Triple A was telling us we had to travel if we were even *thinking* of going to Lancaster. Whenever he wanted to suggest a stop, he took another rubber stamp—a bull's eye—and after he plunged it onto the green stamp pad, he really pressed down with all his considerable girth on the handle of the stamp to make sure the bull's eye landed prominently just where he, the embodiment of the Triple A, wanted—no, required—us to stop. When finally Stumpy had reached the last map in the pile, he used the red pad to stamp the words "End of Journey" on a weird amoeba-like shape with the word "Lancaster" written above it. He bound the leaflets together with a machine that frightened me as I watched him push down yet again with that same considerable girth; as I watched from my seat, the machine nearly flipped over onto the floor, but he managed to catch the TripTik in his hands and hand it like a Communion wafer to my grandfather (who, being a Jew, was not familiar with Communion wafers anyway).

Armed with our TripTik, my grandparents, my brother and I set off on that clammy Saturday morning, when the mist still hung like cotton gauze over the rising sun. We had not eaten breakfast because, as my grandfather proudly announced, "the road passes by a world-famous diner." Many other diners—but surely not world-famous ones—were passed right by as my grandfather drove south (though something told me, as we crossed the George Washington Bridge, that we must have been going north), and it was only two hours later when we came to the first green circle on the TripTik, some immense barn-like structure called the "Red Apple Rest Stop." The parking lot was nearly empty, but there were two or three trailers parked next to one another. "You see, Lena, this is a good place because the truck drivers eat here. They always know where the best food is." Perhaps they, too, had TripTiks that told them to stop there; after all, a huge blue emblem emblazoned with the words "AAA Approved" was affixed to the front door.

I remember my grandmother saying, as we drove away from the Red Apple Rest Stop, that the apple-cured sausage was the best she had ever had. I had no idea what apple-cured sausage was, nor do I think I know what it is today. Whatever the case, I remember that she smacked her lips with happiness and that I hadn't seen her say something nice or complimentary to my grandfather in a long time. That memory, of course, is indelibly connected to the stumpy turpentine-smelling man in the toupee and his TripTik, without which, I was to learn years later, we would have taken the much less boring and considerably more direct route to Lancaster, but not seen my grandmother smile and smack her lips over the taste of the apple-cured sausage.

Sometimes going north in order to go south is worth the trouble. Sometimes it is even the best way to go.

※

My second experience with TripTiks and triptychs was purely accidental and involved a misspelling. I was taking the obligatory Eurail Pass tour of Europe that all college freshmen of my generation would take in the decades before the Euro made Europe inaccessible to poor students, long before the threat of terrorism changed even an experience as innocent, genteel and tentative as second-class train odyssey into a life-or-death decision. I was in Antwerp or Brussels—no, wait, maybe it was Venice, because I have a flashback to Madonna dell'Orto—and I was drawn into the dark nave of a cathedral, as was my wont that particular summer. Once inside, blinded by the darkness until my pupils dilated, I noticed a dim pre-noon sun piercing through the stained glass windows and illuminating the tripartite altarpiece which, if memory serves me correctly, had been painted by Hieronymus Bosch (or Tiziano). The center panel featured the Nativity atop a mountain erupting with the fruitfulness of commerce: there were greengrocers, and fishmongers, and piles of potatoes and apples, a crowd of humanity in bucolic chaos; the cottages and trees encircling them were set against mountains that might have had snow on their peaks, if only they had been in Tyrol rather than Bethlehem. In the bottom right-hand corner, there was a little boxed-off scene, of the Crucifixion—almost an afterthought, or perhaps a foreshadowing of what was to come. The characters in the divine drama were all painted to scale, but somehow the juxtaposed scenes did not mesh well.

On the left panel, almost veiled by the darkness, was an awe-inspiring vision of the Final Judgment and the descent of the damned souls into Hell. The flexed muscles, agonized facial contortions and pure darkness of an abyss that one entered through the open jaws of Beelzebub did not inspire my embryonic faith as much as it caused me to obsess over each and every tortured inch of the painting, in much the same way that one finds it impossible to divert one's glance, hard as one tries, from a fatal multiple car accident or an infomercial about kitchen knives that cut through steel.

Finally, on the right panel, there was a single giant figure of St. Sebastian the martyr, his six-pack abs pierced by arrows, wearing the skimpiest of loincloths, his buff body firm and unyielding against the deadly onslaught. It seemed, at first glance, out of place, more an advertisement for a gentlemen's sauna in Amsterdam than an invitation for prayer and meditation.

I tarried in the nave of that dark cathedral for a good long while as I pondered the three different images from one of the cold wooden pews—and also because it was hot outside and cool inside, and my train for wherever my next stop was would not leave for another three hours. What did the Nativity have to do with Sebastian being pierced by arrows because he chose to love and serve the Lord? And how does the Final Judgment fit chronologically into the tale; should it not have been on the right panel rather than the left? As I recall, I sat staring at the panels so long that I almost lost that next train. As I got up to walk out, I noticed, on the table near the baptismal font, a brochure with a picture of the altarpiece on it. A rusty metal box in front of a candle and chained to the leg of the table silently begged for donations for the brochure. I dropped in a coin—was it 500 lire or 5 francs?—and I read about the famous "tryptich" by Hieronymus Bosch or Tiziano. Three panels that tell a story, but not necessarily from left to right or in chronological order. A complete story that you may have to read, like Chinese, from top to bottom, or like Arabic, from right to left. Parts are left out, details are missing, some extraneous items pop up here and there, but after a moment or two of serene reflection on the three panels together, you are meant to get the picture very clearly.

"*Tryptich*? T-r-y-p-t-i-c-h?" I murmured to myself, then snorted a giggle as I thought back to the long way we took to Lancaster in 1971 because of another TripTik. "So the Triple A spelled it wrong? Fucking idiots."

I turned back to face the altar and glanced peripherally at the baptismal font. It was empty, save for a small glass bowl containing what I guessed to be an ounce or two of holy water. I remember shaking my head from side to side, as if someone had just told me something that made me pity him, and by pure instinct, I dipped my fingers into the cold water and made the sign of the cross on my own forehead: *"Ego te baptizo in nomine Patris, et Filii, et Spiritus Sancti. Amen."*

And as I walked out of the church into a late summer afternoon in Brussels, Antwerp or maybe even Venice, I thought again of the little green arrows on my grandfather's road map, and the stubby man in the toupee extracting his pants from the crack of his behind, and thought, oddly, of apple-cured sausage. Just then it came to me: The church spelled it wrong too. As a student of classics, I knew that *triptych* was a Greek word meaning "folded three times," and the classical Greek word for three, τρεις, does not contain any equivalent of the English letter *y*. The first syllable of *triptych* must, I then reasoned, be spelled like other English words derived from Greek: *triple, triplex, triploid, triploblastic* (note: I didn't know that last word when I made my obligatory Eurail trip to Europe in the summer of 1980, but just thought of it now). I looked it up in an English dictionary that I found in a bookstore as I walked back to the youth hostel. I remember shaking my head for at least the second time that day: "It's not *tryptich*, but *triptych* …T-R-I-P-T-Y-C-H. Jesus, doesn't the Church have editors who proofread?"

The proofreading of what you have in your hands could not be entrusted to anyone else, much less the Church …especially not the Church. The painstaking review of the text of this book—which is revolutionary, apocalyptic or prurient, depending on whom one asks—had to be done out of sequence, as is the case with any other revealed scripture. In this case, though, this "review" turned out to be a time-consuming process of assembling seemingly disparate parts rather than a mere task with a clearly defined beginning, middle and end. In the final analysis, I have spent the last twenty-seven years preparing *Triptych* for dissemination to the public, praying every time I crossed an international border that my handwritten notes—and when fountain pens gave way to technology, my laptop—would not be seized.

What, you may ask, took so much time? After all, this is not a long book, as books go, and only half of its contents were written—more accurately, channeled—by me. The answer is simply that it could not have been done any faster because the three parts of the book took the full twenty-seven years to fall into place.

I first saw the second part, *The Revelation of Anakum*, in Asunción, Paraguay, at siesta time, in the dank bedroom with black velvet curtains of a recently departed friend. Dr. José Ignacio Goma—who had no *segundo appellido* because he was an illegitimate child at a time and in a country where such things mattered—was an attorney who never practiced law, but who achieved social and professional success by marrying the only daughter of a four-star general in the Paraguayan Army. During the Stroessner era, this status afforded my friend and his forebears certain rare and, one might say, enviable privileges. First, his marriage, though sanctified in the Church, was a purely contractual arrangement, which was ideal for Goma because he was more drawn to prepubescent boys than to adult women accustomed to the kowtowing that came along with being born into the top brass of the Paraguayan military. Second, shortly after his son's marriage, Goma's father, Francisco, who had languished for years as a functionary in the Ministry of Foreign Affairs, found himself catapulted to the post of Consul General in Florianópolis, a Brazilian resort that hosted substantial traffic in Paraguayan imports and exports, as well as a lively and unrestrained gay beach scene. Finally, and most importantly, because Goma lived off the generous stipend provided by his father-in-law, he did not have to worry about earning a living, and could devote his time to pursuits he truly enjoyed, such as assembling the largest library of Guaraní literature in the Western Hemisphere, an endeavor that became an obsession and which sent him on regular book-buying junkets all over the globe.

On the October afternoon in question—the temperature in Asunción had soared to 37 degrees Celsius with the humidity hovering at a stifling 80 percent—Goma and I were napping in his ridiculously air-conditioned bedroom: he in a hammock set up on a steel stand in the nearest corner, right under the air conditioner, and I in the queen-sized bed. Goma was thumbing through a magazine, and I could see from the cover facing me that it was some Brazilian porn rag. From the time he first met me in New York, where his father had come to undergo a cancer operation, Goma was enchanted with my interest and proficiency in his native language, Guaraní, which I had learned during my year in the Peace Corps and while teaching English to a group of Paraguayan diplomats at the United Nations.

He used to try to stump me by asking me the meanings of what he thought were unusual words, and when I knew them, he would shift to vulgar colloquialisms, which I typically did not know. He bragged to all his friends, even to his wife, about my knowledge of their language: "*¡Qué rara espécimen es este yanqui! Además, es muy peligroso!*"

During that particular siesta, peering over the top of his porn rag, he asked me, "*Mamopa remanosé?*"[1]

Half asleep, I rolled over, shoved my glasses onto the bridge of my nose, and scowled back, "Heavy, don't you think?"

Goma started laughing uncontrollably, turning bright red and coughing so hard that he had to jump out of the hammock. With his magazine still in hand, he came near my bed: "David, most Paraguayans would answer, *amanosé la camión tuyacuéicha...taco ari*"[2]. Still coughing, but sipping at the *tereré* that I kept on my nightstand, Goma then explained that in Guaraní, *taco* can mean "tree-stump" or "vagina." Still mystified about what had made Goma erupt in such a fit of laughter, but still too much of a prude to enjoy his love of vulgarisms, I asked, "*Ha nde?*"[3]

"*Mba'e? Mo'o amanosépa?*"[4].

"*Néi.*"[5]

He flipped the magazine open to the picture of an extremely well-endowed Brazilian boy with a set of earrings

---

[1] "Where do you want to die?"

[2] More or less, "I want to die like a tireless old truck, propped up on a tree-stump."

[3] "And you?"

[4] "What? Where do I want to die?"

[5] "Yes."

and a tattoo of the Sacred Heart of Jesus that covered half his chest. His skin was the color of cappuccino and his hair was jet black. "Heavy!"

It annoyed me to high heaven when Goma placed the accent on the final syllable. "What?"

"Heavy, heavy. *¿Por qué reniegas de aprender las palabras más importantes del guaraní, mi querido?*"[6] He began to laugh and cough again. "*Hevi, hevi pora...amanosé hevime.*"[7]

I shook my head and buried it again in my damp pillow, which was now freezing. Goma finished coughing, and the room suddenly became silent and oppressive. He walked over to the bed, hoping, I imagine, that I would say something because Goma hated silence. When I did not take the bait, he announced, "David, are you up? Come, I want to show you something."

I followed him to the bookcase in the corner of the bedroom, which was neatly packed with books in Guaraní. He pulled one out, a leather bound volume chipping along the spine...a book that had not been opened in at least a century. "I just found this in Buenos Aires. It's a dictionary of our language published in Rio de Janeiro, believe it or not, in 1878." He was buttering me up by calling Guaraní "our language." I hated his obsession with sex, but he was in the final analysis a loyal friend, someone who took me into his confidence and in whom, I think, I could confide; therefore, I shook off my momentary anger and gingerly took the book into my hands, but I

---

[6]"Why do you refuse to learn the most important Guaraní words, my dear?"

[7]"His ass, his beautiful ass...I want to die in his ass."

didn't want to risk cracking the leather further by opening it.

"And what about this one?" He picked out the only yellow paperback in the entire book case. One could tell that it had been read many times because the cover was frayed, and the edges of the pages were gray with years of hand grease and thumbprints. He opened it to a page that had some notes in the margin. "*Rehechámapa?*"[8]

"*Mba'e co cuatiaarandú rera?*"[9]

"*La Revelación de Anakum,* published right here in Asunción in the early 80s."

I had never heard of it. "Is it a novel?"

"No, no, no. Nothing of the sort, *che ra'a.*[10] It's a religious book, concerning a new prophecy to a man...Anakum...who must have come from here because it's written in our Guaraní. Well, mostly Spanish, but some Guaraní here and there, in the important parts." For that fleeting moment, I took pride in how well I had taught him to speak properly in English.

"Can I read it?"

For the first time, I saw fright writ large across his devil-may-care face. "Here, in this room, yes. But, you can't take it out of the room."

I remember thinking to myself: *How bizarre, is he for real?* "Is it hard to understand?"

"For you, *mi querido,* no." He winked. "Because the Guaraní has all been translated into Spanish." Again he erupted into laughs and coughs.

---

[8] "Have you seen it?"

[9] "What's the name of this book?"

[10] "my friend"

I read the *Revelación* that night, and the next, and nearly forgot about it until one night, in 1996, when I saw the same yellow book sitting on a bookshelf in an Andean handicrafts shop along Calle Linares (alternately called "Gringo Alley") in the Witches' Market in La Paz, Bolivia. I pointed and asked if it was for sale, but the shopkeeper, an Aymara woman with a bowler cap and a mouthful of coca leaves, moved her head from side to side. *"El libro no se vende, señor, pero las telas sí."*[11]

I never thought that the *Revelation of Anakum* was anything other than one of innumerable latter-day prophecies until the Supreme Court rendered its decision in *Vance v. Warden* in the final days before the summer recess in 2004. When that momentous decision—which is reproduced in the third part of this book—was announced, and I noticed who the petitioner's attorneys had been, I remembered that particular siesta in Asunción with Goma, whom I had not seen or heard from in years. An intense Internet research revealed eventually that he had died in 1999 of a heart attack during a visit to Curitiba. Feeling sorrowful at having lost a friend, even a long-estranged one, the memory of Goma led me to break with personal tradition by reaching out to rekindle more recent friendships: first with my classmate, Andrew Sear (who, actually, had never been a friend, but an acquaintance, and a fairly anal retentive one at that) and then with my professor of constitutional law, Dylan Hardwick. In certain ways, life had been unkind to both of them—Andy had been hired and shortly thereafter "invited to look elsewhere" by two of the major blue-blood firms in New Orleans, and Professor

---

[11] "This book is not for sale, but the fabrics are."

Hardwick was exhibiting the incipient signs of Parkinson's Disease just as his marriage was cruising through its death throes—but I detected in their e-mails to me a remarkable fortitude of spirit that had been absent when I first came to know them in law school, back in the days when they were supercilious libertines (I wanted to write "haughty pricks," but they have become friends and thought it more decorous not to insult them in print.). The three of us met only twice in the course of a single week in November 2004, and in those eight or ten hours perched over Sazeracs served in plastic cups at a dodgy joint called the Kitty Kat Korner in the residential antechamber of the French Quarter, the two of them revealed to me the amazing story of how they became involved in defending Ed Vance. With the sting of those cocktails still on my tongue, and feeling spry and nimble for the first time since law school, I left for La Paz, Bolivia, where I checked into the Hotel Europa and in ten days typed out the first part of the book, *The Art of Correction*.

Frankly, since that week in La Paz in November 2004, I have been debating with myself whether to publish this book or simply to stash it away somewhere it can never be found—a safe deposit box or behind the dust-covered law books on my bookshelves. Certain books have power, and that power, if not wielded correctly or by the right persons, can be dangerous. In the end, I decided that I had nothing more to lose. There is a reason that I came across the *Revelation of Anakum*, a reason why I reconnected with Andy and Professor Hardwick, a reason why they chose me as the person in whom they would confide, a reason why certain Supreme Court decisions are suppressed. Faith never came easily to me, but the truth has to come out eventually, and even if I am risking prosecution under some overly broad antiterrorism law for letting the word out, I must, in the end, answer to myself and to God.

Part One

THE ART OF CORRECTION

THE ART OF CORRECTION

One

For Edwin Francis Vance, life was as good as it gets—or at least that was the predominant view around town. He was young, blond, athletic and so surreally handsome that people meeting him for the first time often wondered whether he was human or merely the cruel mirage of some sexual fantasy gone haywire. As soon as word had infiltrated Uptown's beauty salons that the Crescent City finally had in its midst a *true* Adonis who was neither a homosexual nor an alumnus of Jesuit High School (the two all too often being interchangeable), flocks of fading debutantes started crossing the proverbial tracks to consult Ed on getting better rates for their—and more often their husbands'—car insurance. Within six months of its opening, his garage-sized insurance brokerage on the southeastern wing of a strip mall on Gentilly Boulevard could easily be, and occasionally was, confused with that of Dr. Cerise, the gynecologist two doors down.

Other men might have been flattered by all the attention, but not Ed. No, no—not Ed. Though invariably polite, and even anachronistically chivalrous, to the women who patronized him, he committed the unforgivable sin of never reciprocating, even in jest, any of their multiple ministrations or flirtations. In pretty short order, with a combination of regret and revulsion, his self-appointed *Schutzstaffel* of overbleached and oversexed Stepford wives, unable to arrive at any other rational conclusion save that Ed Vance just *had to be* gay, retreated back over the tracks whence they came.

This did not stop the chatter, however—for New Orleans, after all, could not stop being New Orleans—and when a male manicurist on the corner of Green and Panola all the way Uptown, right near the bend in the river, overheard Charleen Denegre lament that she "should have realized no guy as drop-dead gorgeous as Ed Vance could be straight" (to which her big-haired sister-in-law Madeleine sighed, "oh my, what a waste of the cutest bubble butt in all of Orleans Parish," a comment that even Charleen couldn't quite understand), a new wave of insurance seekers rapidly took form. Initially, two or three male prospectors—individually, not in pack formation—made the trek from the Faubourg Marigny to verify the rumors, and when these two or three broadcast the encouraging results of their field research to the fellow patrons of the matching pair of gay bars on Bourbon and Dumaine, a veritable exodus from the Quarter to the no-man's land in Gentilly broke loose.

As September gave way to October, the new surge of insurance patrons grew larger because, in contrast to his apparent indifference to female clients, Ed reveled in satisfying the insurance needs, if not the erotic fantasies, of his male admirers. Some, who were suspicious by nature, even wondered whether Ed did not go out of his way to whet their appetites by his suggestive attire. "Ed Vance ain't nothing but a pretty boy cocktease, that's how I see it," proclaimed Anton Davis as he held court, smugly sipping his apple martini at the Kitty Kat Korner, one of the Quarter's less reputable establishments. But what Anton and the other spurned members of New Orleans' gay posse totally misread was that Ed, however suggestive his attire might be, never made any conscious effort to adapt to *them*; rather, *they* were being drawn—by lust or curiosity, though mostly lust—to conform to *him*. For, true to his nature as a progressive, Ed Vance had never owned a suit and shunned the conventionality of a necktie, preferring to arrive at his office every morning at precisely 8:17 wearing a red or black muscle shirt tucked into one of his dozen pairs of skin-tight blue jeans, waist 31, which hugged the cheeks of his well-sculpted butt as if the man and Levi's had been created for one another. He might as well have been one of the Kitty Kat Korner's patrons.

One particular day, November 1st, had not been any different. In New Orleans, most offices were closed in observance of All Saints' Day, but Ed knew from experience that a Holy Day of Obligation would hardly deter his faithful customers in the least. There had been a time, years before, when Ed would have closed his office and foregone work on All Saints' Day. But that was the past, when he had been a Roman Catholic. Now, Ed Vance, who had more than once in his adolescence toyed with the idea of becoming a priest, and had even spent the summer after his sophomore year in college building a schoolhouse with Opus Dei in rural El Salvador, was knowingly and intentionally committing a moral sin so that he could tend to his gay flock.

As predicted, business had been a bit brisker than normal that day, if for no other reason than that Ed had lost the first forty-five minutes scraping dried eggs and soap off the front window of his office. The first of his male admirers to arrive, Marc Alfortis, begged for the right to clean the window for him, but Ed refused with a grateful arm around the shoulder, which made Marc shudder with goosebumps. "I guess those kids had to give me a trick once they figured out they couldn't extract any treats except some insurance brochures and a couple of dusty old swimming trophies." Another man, a mere mortal, might have let himself get distracted by such a puerile prank, but Ed Vance was no ordinary man. He had finally reached the stage of which others merely dreamt: unadulterated, undiluted comfort.

Boy, I have so much to be thankful for.

Once the other lights in the strip mall had dimmed, and the stream of handsome gay gym worshippers had gone dry for the day, Ed did the same thing he did every other evening. As with most things about Ed, his movements were more predictable and precise than any Swiss watch on the market. First, he looked at himself in the mirror and used a disposable razor to even off his sideburns. He could never tolerate scruff, whether on his neck or anywhere on his face, and he had one of his clients, a hair stylist from the other end of the shopping mall, even out his hairline every afternoon after lunch. Then Ed lightly ran his fingers through his smooth blond hair, guiding the wavy locks over his scalp until they draped down naturally over his temples. This was a task of extreme delicacy, and if he fiddled with his hair for a second too long, the desired effect might be irretrievable. Once satisfied that he again appeared debonair but focused, he smiled broadly at his reflection to make sure there were no remnants of the afternoon's California roll from Yoshi Sushi stuck between his teeth and sauntered over to the front door to turn off the overhead lights as well as the neon sign flashing his name above the storefront.

With only the glare of the parking-lot street lamp guiding him from behind, Ed returned to sit at his metal desk. There, he closed his eyes and, cupping his head in his hands, inhaled and exhaled, slowly and gently, as if he were counting the molecules of oxygen going in and the molecules of carbon dioxide going out. This lasted exactly twenty-four seconds. Then, reaching into the bottom left-hand drawer, he pulled out a thumb-worn yellow paperback. Using the bookmark to flip it open, he propped the book up on the stapler that now horizontally dissected the circle of pale fluorescent light buzzing from his desk lamp. Hunching over the book like a Talmudic scholar, he began to read intently, raising his head to the dark ceiling after every sentence or two and murmuring the words to himself. When at last he heard the old blue Mazda owned by the notions shop cashier drive off—a bit more than half an hour later—he reverently returned the book to its drawer, locked it, shut off the desk lamp and walked out again into the dank New Orleans night.

As a matter of habit and preference, Ed avoided the Interstate and took Gentilly Boulevard straight upriver, past the Fairgrounds, until it fed into Broad Street. Never exceeding the speed limit, even to make it through a yellow light, he passed the street he needed and hung a sharp U-turn in the appropriate lane so that he could make a perfectly legal right onto Esplanade heading down to the French Quarter. In one detail, though, that evening was different. When he reached Burgundy, instead of coasting through to Canal, he stopped at the corner of Ursulines Street for about ten seconds, just long enough for his girl-friend Josephine to hop down the front steps of her modest Creole cottage. Her massive Persian earrings tugged at her small earlobes, and her long jet-black pigtails were piled up into a haphazard bun. Because she knew that it would please Ed, she was wearing the extravagantly flowery *huipil* that he had brought her back from Yucatán. Even in the darkness, she might have been taken for Frida Kahlo's reincarnation (except that Josephine had no limp).

Once buckled into the front seat of Ed's Accord, Josephine leaned over to peck him on the lips, and Ed resumed the routine: first a left turn on Canal, then a right onto Magazine, ambling past Poydras and the federal courts up to Louisiana Avenue. Had he continued straight up the road, he would have arrived at his front door in four minutes, assuming there had been no red light at Washington Avenue. Instead, like every other autumn day, he turned left at Louisiana and then right onto Tchoupitoulas. He was well aware of the futility of this daily detour along the river because he knew that Hansen's was still closed for the season, but somehow he could not bring himself to abandon the hope of surprising his kids with an extra-large nectar cream Sno-Bliz.

As he drove past Hansen's weather-beaten white shack, where he had spent many a summer night waiting an hour or even more for Papa Hansen to shave ice and Miss Mary to drench it in her homemade syrup, he smacked his lips and exclaimed to Josephine, "Boy, Josephine, how I wish they would stay open all year; I would even volunteer to help out in the evenings!"

"So would I, as long as it meant being with you..." With those words, the first she had spoken since sitting beside him that night, she bowed her head down to the gear shift to kiss his right hand.

Ed pulled into a strip mall far less dated than the one in which he worked, and parked in front of Baskin & Robbins. "I'll be back in a jiffy," he said with a smile, returning about six minutes later with a pint of chocolate chocolate chip, another of pralines and cream, and a quart of "gourmet" pistachio (which is how he referred to any pistachio ice cream that had actual nuts in it). It wasn't Halloween any more, but he had treats to distribute, and this accentuated Ed's natural ebullience.

When he pulled up in front of his shotgun on Annunciation Street, three houses from the corner of Austerlitz, he leaned over Josephine to witness the familiar rustle behind the curtains of his living room window.

"Daddy, daddy, daddy..."

Two miniature silhouettes bestrode the now open doorway: His eldest son Sammy, aged seven, and Jonathan, aged five. Had the two brothers not differed in height by at least a head and a half, they might have been mistaken for twins. Ed put his white bag of treats down on the porch and swung both boys up into his outstretched arms, squeezing them to his smooth, neatly peppered cheeks and smothering them alternately with kisses.

"I love you, love you, love you, yes yes I love you, love you, love you."

Truly gallant (even when he found it necessary to belch and put a napkin to his lips), he bowed to Josephine and waved her across the threshold. Grasping the Baskin & Robbins bag with one hand and his two sons' tiny hands with the other, he entered the climate-controlled comfort of his favorite place on earth.

Yes, on this particular November 1st, it was hot in New Orleans.

He was eight minutes later than usual, but Stella, his wife, knew that he had stopped to buy ice cream.

What a creature of habit!

Stella thought her husband's predictability was cute, and sometimes during sex, which they still had twice a day despite nine years of marriage, she would whisper into his ears how huge a turn-on this particular character trait was. She came out of the kitchen in her apron holding their two-year-old daughter, Rachel, fast against her breasts. Without missing a beat, Stella glanced with a cordial smile at the one person in the room whom she did not yet know, and kissed Ed on the lips single-mindedly, as if for two or three seconds her entire mind and the world itself had vanished, and only her love for her husband, and his love for her, had ever existed since the beginning of time and for-ever and ever, world without end, amen.

"Honey, I'm so glad you made it home safely. You didn't tell me we were having company."

"Yes, you're right, my love, but I wanted to surprise you. Josephine Colette, I want to introduce you to the light of my life, my beautiful, beloved wife, Stella."

The two women took each other's hands and pecked each another mechanically, not with any feeling but not with resentment either, once on each cheek. "Please, Josephine, make yourself at home. You'll just have to ex-cuse me for a few minutes because I want to make sure the stuffed artichokes don't overcook. They're Ed's favorite, you know, and they're prone to burning. Thankfully I made two or three extra." Each of her stuffed artichokes weighed at least a pound, and she was mighty proud of that fact; her grandmother Estelle had taught her well. She clapped her hands together, and smiled at her hus-band. "Come on, Sammy, Jonathan, take your little sister back to the bedroom and play, just keep it down to a mild ricochet."

Keep it down to a mild ricochet.

This was one of Stella's hallmark expressions. Each time Ed heard these words—and he might hear her say them six or seven times a day—he would feel anew rumbling through every inch of his being the electric hum of a love so immense and so immutable that tears would well up in the corners of his deep hazel eyes and his Adam's apple would rise and fall with the contraction of his throat.

How lucky I am to be in love with a woman who saw it fit to marry someone like me, a dreamer!

As her husband stared with adoration into her eyes, Stella felt a tinge of embarrassment because of their guest. "Honey, will you go open up a bottle of wine?"

"Yes, the best wine we have, sweetheart, 'cause we'z a celebratin' tonight." He made a humping gesture with his arms and hips, which made Stella laugh, and while disco-shuffling his way to the television cabinet, he made her laugh even louder by shrieking the verse "push push in the bush" in a Ninth Ward twang.

Ed knelt down and dug behind the video cassettes to retrieve a bottle of 1982 Château Margaux *premier cru* which one of his appreciative voyeur clients had given to him as a Christmas gift the previous year. "Stella, darling, please bring out three wine glasses…you know, the nice crystal ones we keep for special guests." He smiled at Josephine, who was still standing in the same spot she occupied when she had entered.

"And the corkscrew too…don't forget the corkscrew. Just make sure it's the easy one." He heard the water in the kitchen stop running, then, turning to Josephine, he smiled and said, "She'll be right back in. In the meantime, please sit down anywhere you like and make yourself at home."

At first, Ed struggled with the lead wrapper over the cork because he had just had a manicure that afternoon, but as soon as he managed to scrape out a flake, the rest came peeling off in an unbroken spiral. As Stella stepped back into the room balancing a silver tray with three Bordeaux glasses and the easy corkscrew, Josephine was still nodding her admiration at Ed's prodigy.

He poured a bit of wine into his glass and, with much flourish, sniffed the bouquet. "Hmmm…wild blackberries, cedar flakes, and a hint of peppery cinnamon." Both women giggled, and Ed looked back with a boyish frown to let them know he was trying to sound epicurean and erudite. He swirled the wine around the glass—"nice even legs"—and slurped it all into his gullet, loudly swooshing the amber-red liquid back and forth like mouthwash through his perfectly aligned teeth.

Ed looked up at the chandelier and, in a disastrously bad British accent, delivered the verdict: "Let's see…well, the tannins are a bit dry and harsh at first, but all in all it has a somewhat buttery finish."

The women smiled silently for fear of appearing to question Ed's oenophilic expertise. Stella beamed with pride: "Ed really knows his wine."

Standing opposite the two women, Ed filled a glass for his wife, then one for Josephine, and lastly his own, which he raised with his right hand. Stella peered into his beautiful hazel eyes, which were focused on her and her alone.

"I'd like to make a toast to both of you. Stella, I'm so glad you're finally meeting Josephine because I intend to have my next child with her…hopefully more than one. So, cheers to you both. *Tupã ñanderehe.*"

A calliope on the Mississippi broke the nighttime stillness in response to Ed's toast, but Stella's glass shattered as it hit the hardwood floor. In the split second it took for Ed to clink his glass against Josephine's, a million thoughts, none of them sweet or charitable, bombarded the saccharine Stella's mind:

You self-righteous prick, who the hell do you think you are to treat me like your whore?

How dare you bring this two-bit slut here and rub your indiscretions in my face!

What kind of a lowlife sticks his kids' faces in his own shit?

But, she couldn't voice them. She wouldn't dare. She too knew the rules, all too well. As her new mind struggled to swing back into equilibrium so that she could formulate a *useful* response, she caught a side glimpse of Josephine still sipping her wine and smiling coquettishly at Ed. Yes, Ed, Stella's husband. *What a fucking skank.* At that moment, Stella's faith—admittedly not yet as nurtured or evolved as Ed's, but faith nonetheless—cracked ever so slightly, and one of those million jumbled thoughts percolating in the recess of her atavistic, unevolved subconscious squeezed through the fissure before she could capture it.

"How can you hate me so much?"

At this point, Ed excused himself, wiped his lips with a linen napkin and went into the kitchen.

"Stella, honey, please come in here."

Ed was standing at the far end of the kitchen with his back to the two women, for Josephine—perhaps out of curiosity, perhaps out of not wanting to be left alone—had responded to Ed's summons as well. At five foot eleven, he had to stretch just a bit to pull out the black velvet correcting cloth from the cabinet above the refrigerator.

"Stella, are you in comfort?" His voice was even, emotionless. He might have been asking, "Do you like the wine?"

With Josephine at her side like a sister in battle, Stella stared straight ahead, through the window above the sink, at the birdbath in their matchbox of a backyard. "Yes."

"Please assume the position, Stella."

She knelt down with her face to the oven door, and did not utter any protest or ask any question because she could think of nothing useful. Ed carefully draped the correcting cloth over his wife's head so that she resembled a Muslim woman in the middle of the first prostration of the *'Isha* prayer. He then bent down himself to open the cabinet beneath the sink to retrieve the *molcajete* that Stella had once or twice used to mash avocados for homemade guacamole. *It's unblemished and unconsecrated, so why not?* So she had thought at the time she made the guacamole, even though she realized fully well that Ed probably would have found her vulgar use of this precious object somewhat sacrilegious.

Their *molcajete*, chiseled out of black volcanic rock, was just a bit larger than an adult bowling ball. Ed and Stella had bought it a few years back for the gringo price of a hundred pesos at a stall in the *Mercado La Sonora* in Mexico City, and when he was spotted ceremoniously carrying it through international arrivals in Houston on their return, two overzealous U.S. Customs agents, thinking he might be hiding something, took him into a booth for a random strip search in which, yes, the dark Hispanic one did ask Ed to spread his butt cheeks.

✳

Ed struck his prostrating wife Stella three times on the back of the head with the *molcajete*. Between each blow, in a calm and calibrated voice, he recited the following two verses: "Speak truthfully and knowingly. Only ask questions that the person to whom they are posed can answer truthfully and knowingly."

After the third blow, Stella tumbled to the side, and Ed, who had not even broken a sweat because the intensity of the blows had been as strictly calibrated as the recitations, felt for a pulse at her carotid artery. Finding none, he stood up, smoothing down his skin-tight size 31 Levi's, and led Josephine by the hand back to the living room. In silence, they continued drinking their Bordeaux and munching on macadamia nuts as Sammy and Jonathan were audibly enjoying their ice cream and playing with little Rachel in the second bedroom. Ed finished his second glass of Château Margaux and, seeing the bottle was now empty, announced, "That's enough for one night, I think."

He turned to kiss Josephine on the cheek and walked over to the telephone, fishing the shards of crystal out of the pool of wine next to the coffee table. Then, after washing his hands in the kitchen sink and carefully wiping them on a neatly-ironed dishtowel, he called 911 from the wall-mounted telephone. As matter-of-factly as if he were ordering a pizza, he told the operator: "My name is Ed Vance, and I live at 4006 Annunciation Street, between Austerlitz and Constantinople. I have corrected my wife Stella. She is no longer breathing. If it's not too much bother, please have someone come by to take her away."

When three New Orleans policemen and a medical team arrived some forty minutes later, they found Ed washing out the two remaining Bordeaux glasses, and Josephine wiping them dry, in the kitchen. The *molcajete*, barely stained by a fine spray of blood that had spurted out of the point of impact as Stella tumbled to the side, was resting on the counter, but the black velvet correcting cloth was still in place over the back of Stella's skull. Her body was in a fetal position, the ends of her silky hair matted down in the shallow halo of viscous scarlet that now engulfed her head.

After Ed had been arrested and led in handcuffs out of the house, the forensic team conducted a thorough search of the house during which they found traces of finely ground coca leaves and a box of sodium bicarbonate on the coffee table. From atop the microwave, they also seized and marked as evidence a sealed one-hundred bag box of *mate de coca* which Ed and Stella had picked up at the duty-free shop in La Paz, Bolivia. The receipt was stuck under a New Orleans Saints magnet on the refrigerator door.

Stella Carruthers Vance was pronounced dead on arrival at Southern Baptist Hospital. She had just turned thirty. The autopsy, hastily conducted by the Orleans Parish Medical Examiner, concluded that the cause of death was not exsanguination, but a cerebral hemorrhage resulting from a massive and sustained head trauma.

Two

It was barely 7:15 in the morning, and Judge Patrick Mc-Carthy's day had already gotten off to a miserable start. His massive, puffy, red fingers clutched and squeezed the steering wheel of his 1988 Lincoln Continental as if he were dangling from the top ledge of a skyscraper, and every time he hit a red light, he bashed the wheel a few times and cursed aloud. He was, as his wife was wont to say, "fit to be tied."

Fucking school zones.

He should have known better than to go into work today. About four hours earlier, the shrill buzz of his black rotary-dial telephone had shaken him out of a nightmare in which he found himself walking naked along the streetcar tracks on St. Charles Avenue, all alone but for the sea of ferrets engulfing him, shimmying to and fro and nibbling at his waterlogged red ankles and clawing along the varicose-veined trail up his fleshy calves.

"Hello, Patrick. Sorry to disturb you this early, but it's an emergency."

He was drenched in sweat, and though he thrust his palms down blindly on the nightstand to find his glasses so that he could assure himself that he was in fact no longer in the realm of dreams, he immediately recognized the husky, breathless voice, and this prevented him from screaming expletives into the receiver.

Sharae LaRoche was a single mother of four who had decided one day ten years ago to push herself away from the public trough and plunge head-first into the dicey undercurrents of New Orleans politics, thereby acquiring a private meal ticket that would not have to be divvied up so many ways. She was currently serving as the eminently visible and outspoken president of the New Orleans City Council, quite an achievement for a woman who had dropped out of high school after becoming pregnant at age fourteen and could still barely read at an eighth-grade level.

"Hold on, let me get a pencil to write this down." Judge McCarthy hated mornings, and he hated even more being awoken before dawn to dispense what he euphemistically called "party favors." *Mother fucker, where are the goddamned pencils…I can put a whole friggin' box here next to me at night, and they'll vanish into the fucking air before I wake up. Jesus fucking Christ.* "Hold on, will ya?" he screamed into the phone which he jolted against the faux marble tabletop.

Now I've gotta get outta bed, and I'll never get back to sleep. Mother fucker!

As he rocked back and forth to gather up enough momentum to throw his stumpy legs off the bed, a ballpoint came peeking out from under the covers. "Now, would you keep your voice down, Einstein, before you wake the whole fucking house up?" His wife was not pleased. She was never pleased. He pried the pen out of his wife Maureen's hand and barked, "Thanks darlin'. Now get the hell back to sleep."

"OK…I'm back, Sharae. Now, what can I do you for?" A groan erupted from beneath the sweat-drenched comforter not only because Maureen detested the vulgarity of being called darlin', but because she knew that her husband was pandering to the black bitch to avoid sounding pissed-off, and he was not soundly convincing at all. But, disguises were an ill fit for Judge McCarthy at any time, much less at 3:10 a.m., and the fact that he, with all his book and street smarts, did not yet know this about himself annoyed his wife even more.

"It's all a set-up, you know how these NOPD cops are, all a bunch of cocksucking racists, Patrick…"

With those words as a preface, Patrick could have finished the tale of woe himself. It seemed that Sharae's eldest son Calvin had been innocently hanging out with some friends at Nickie's Shot-a-Rama, a local institution ironically set two blocks north of the Orleans Parish Criminal District Court, to enjoy some of their ninety-six original cocktails, all of which were listed in alphabetical order on a hand-painted sign suspended above the bar by old bicycle chains and which had obscenely alliterative names like *Anal Ambrosia*, *Jamaican Jerk-Off Juice*, *Cum 4 My Cunt* (a spoof on the old Drifters song "Sweets for My Sweet"), *Prostate Propane* and by far the most revolting, *Queer Quincy's Quince Quark*, which consisted of equal measures of apple schnapps, pear brandy, Galliano and Bailey's Irish Cream. Calvin was halfway through the letter E when a white kid with a backwards-turned baseball cap and baggy jeans came up to him and smiled. Calvin asked him if was looking for some "stuff," and the stupid white kid smiled again and nodded, then went outside. Calvin put his Erection Energizer down on the bar and followed, motioning the kid away from the glow of street lamps and into the pitch black behind the Shot-a-Rama. When Calvin exchanged a pebble of crack for the kid's rolled-up twenty-dollar bill, a shadow stepped out of the darkness, grabbed Calvin's hands and said, "Please put your hands above your head. You're under arrest. You have the right to remain silent…"

Guilty as shit, and she wants me to save his fucking life. What is this now, his third possession WID offense? He's gonna get some ass pounding of his own pretty soon 'cause he'll have to do some hard time at Angola, no fucking way around it.

Contrary to Patrick's expectations, Councilwoman Sharae did not ask him to work his magic so that the District Attorney would drop the charges. That pressure would come later. For now, all she wanted from Patrick was to get her son out of Central Lock-Up on his own recognizance before the bloodhounds from the *Times-Picayune* caught on to this latest of scandals in the LaRoche household.

Patrick promised to do what he could and dialed one of the magistrates, but his home phone was ringing busy, which at 3:30 a.m. meant that he had taken it off the hook. *Smarter than me, I'll tell ya…*

He tried to call another magistrate, for a city like New Orleans couldn't get by on just one, and when that too was unsuccessful, he began to panic. *Look at her sleeping like a baby when I'm pulling my fucking hair out.* "Maureen, who's on call tonight, do you remember?"

No answer.

He tried again to swing himself out of bed, but this time with much more huffing and puffing than before. He rocked the mattress as if he were on a trampoline—intentionally, of course, so that his wife would be sure to wake up. For Judge Patrick McCarthy, getting out of bed was no minor feat: He had poor circulation and pitting edema in his feet and ankles, varicose veins, hypertension, not to mention diabetes, and though he was, at six foot one, the tallest member of the Orleans Parish Criminal District Court by far, he weighed three hundred and ninety-two pounds, or so he claimed. How he arrived at this exact figure was anyone's guess. When Maureen had once challenged him, he began to spout out an explanation so Byzantine that even he himself got confused: "You see, darlin', according to my medical records I weighed three hundred and fifty on...let's see here...June 14, 1993, and if we assume I've been eating twelve hundred excess calories per day since then and not increasing my physical activity, then since a pound of fat has thirty five hundred calories, you gotta multiply twelve hundred by the number of days since the check-up and divide by thirty-five hundred..." Antiseptically mathematical though it sounded, his theory had two small flaws: First, the nurse who weighed him had been writing down three hundred and fifty pounds on his chart for the preceding seven years because that was the maximum capacity of the cardiologist's Detecto scale, and second, Patrick had no justification or back-up data for his "assumption" that he was eating twelve hundred extra calories per day. With his penchant for fried oyster po' boys dressed with pickles and extra butter, the actual figure could have been thirty-six hundred or seventy-two hundred or even more.

She could sleep through a friggin' earthquake, I swear.

The comforter rustled again, and Maureen reluctantly poked her head out this time. Her eyes were still glued shut, her hair as wiry as steel wool in the curlers she had left in. She looked like a hibernating turtle whose hovel had been plowed up by a Caterpillar combine.

"Can't you remember anything? It's Cressich on Tuesday nights. All month long. Jesus…"

✳

Once Patrick had straightened out the problem with Calvin LaRoche, he sank his head back down into the cold, damp pillow, but every time he closed his eyes, he saw himself drowning again in the sea of ferrets who were gnawing away his toes and his other extremities. He tried to block the image out by focusing on what cases would be on the docket later that morning, but for the life of him he could not remember. He never could remember, and he never carried around the pocket calendar that his clerk dutifully prepared for him each Friday. He claimed he enjoyed being spontaneous, but actually he was one of the most disorganized renaissance men in New Orleans.

When Magistrate Judge Cressich called an hour later to tell him that everything had been handled for the moment, Patrick slammed the receiver down and swept the anvil of a phone off his night table onto the floor. The sound of the dial tone pierced the stillness of the rest of the house and blocked out the soothing rumble of the soft Lake Pontchartrain breeze tossing about the palm fronds in their backyard.

"All right, is everybody happy now? Can't even get any sleep around this place. And all this for the measly salary they pay me? Fuck it, now I'm up. Maureen, fix me some eggs and Jimmy Dean sausage patties. Better make it four of each."

"What time is it?" She did not dare pull down the comforter because she knew by the tone of his voice it was going to be a long and very bad day.

"Ten to five, I think. Come on, fix breakfast and I'll get to court early for a change."

"Give me five minutes, OK?"

He was still thinking of what awaited him that morning, and he thought he might derive some sadistic pleasure from calling Magistrate Cressich, who was as anal retentive as they came, and asking him what was on the docket. Something was on the tip of his tongue, but he was repressing it for some reason.

"Maureen, come on, darlin'. Time waits for no man or woman. I'm dying of hunger here, so…" Just then, the memory of what awaited him at court came to him, and he started running his fingers through his thick mop of red hair. How could he have forgotten it? Could things get any worse?

He purposely yelled so that everyone in the house would get up.

"Shit!"

✳

The day went from bad to worse. Patrick was still famished because he hated well-done eggs, and Maureen had left them in the frying pan too long. He liked his eggs one way, and one way only: sunny-side up and a little runny. Then someone had eaten all of the Jimmy Dean sausage patties. He hated the links, and it was obvious that everyone else in the McCarthy home shared his taste because two unopened boxes of maple-smoked sausage links were snowed under in the back of the freezer. She sizzled up a few of them, and he ate them, albeit reluctantly, because they were not what he had wanted; thus, he left the house unsatisfied, and within minutes, he was hungry again. Of necessity, one thought occupied by force the front of his mind because what lay at the back was something he could not deal with just yet.

The Biscuit Barn should be open by now, right?

Despite the gruff Pantagruelian exterior and vulgar language, Judge Patrick McCarthy was, at the heart of it all, a highly sensitive man with a heart of gold. He had wanted at one time to go to seminary and take orders, like most eldest sons in the Irish Channel of his generation, but the condemnation and shame thrust upon him by his confessor after his first episode of premarital sex cured him of any sacerdotal illusions. As he drove along Canal Street, right after looping around Greenwood Cemetery and its foreboding marble gate, his mental images shifted from a sausage-and-cheese biscuit to a man strapped to a gurney and the unfairness of it all. Fourteen individuals—twelve jurors and two alternates—had been empaneled to decide whether to indict Ed Vance for first-degree murder, which, if proven at a subsequent trial beyond a reasonable doubt, carried with it the possibility— no, in New Orleans, the very high *probability*—of the death penalty if a jury of Vance's peers so recommended. These grand jurors presumably swore an oath before God and country to perform their duty conscientiously and impartially, and proceeded to hear the state's evidence from a variety of witnesses whose identities were kept secret in proceedings that were required by the state constitution itself to be kept absolutely secret. Patrick imagined the first witness must have been the Medical Examiner, who would have explained in cold, medical terms how the blow of the *molcajete* to Stella Carruthers Vance's head caused blood to spurt out of the cerebral tissue into her skull cavity like water from a garden faucet filling a balloon on a summer day. The arresting officers also must have shown the grand jury the gruesome photographs of the scene: Stella's body, her silky hair matted down in a pool of her own blood and brain juices, lay stiffly folded in the fetal position next to the stove, as Vance and his paramour sipped wine and nibbled on macadamia nuts in the salon. Vance would have had no opportunity to object or cross examine. The alternates never had a chance: it took the original twelve men and women twenty-one minutes to return a true bill of indictment formally charging Ed Vance with first-degree murder.

Patrick was shaking his head at the woman in Spandex sauntering across Tulane Avenue with a plastic laundry basket, but he was really reacting involuntarily to the shocking result of another mathematical calculation he had just done in his head: *Holy Mother of God, that's not even two minutes per person!*

Before pulling into the judges' parking lot, which, coincidentally or not, was sandwiched in between the court and the prison, he remembered his biscuit, but the Biscuit Barn still had its iron gate in place. He could always go to Nickie's Shot-a-Rama for an eye-opener—in fact, today, he might be able to put one to good use—and if he had, he would have run into his old buddy Professor Dy-

Ian Hardwick, who was killing some time before heading over to Judge McCarthy's courtroom to follow the Vance arraignment.

"Just keep an eye on the public defender they appointed to represent this guy Vance," Judge Hyman had told Professor Hardwick last night, "and let me know if you think he'll do what needs to be done."

In the end, Patrick's hunger for a good, solid breakfast won him over. He could not face the day without some pleasure reinforcement.

He looked at the digital clock above his car radio: 7:28. Parasol's would not unlock its waterlogged green screen door for at least another hour. *Shit, just my luck!* Just then, the morning sun blinked at the gold amulet hanging from his rear-view mirror, and a dash of light shooting off the dot on the Buddha's forehead nearly blinded him. He smiled. Patrick had a voracious appetite for learning about philosophy and especially other religions, and a Zen retreat on which he had gone two years back really left an imprint on him. He had come back refreshed and chomping at the bit to learn more. *How bad can a religion that emulates a fat man be?* The same afternoon, he signed up to audit an undergraduate course on Buddhism at Loyola, but when he showed up for the first lecture, he found that there was no way he could squeeze into any of the elementary-school style pupil's chairs. When one of the sophomores lifted up the tabletop on Patrick's chosen seat, probably out of fear because Patrick vaguely connected the boy's face with a defendant who had pleaded *nolo contendere* on a DUI charge last year, the judge nodded with relief and grinned so broadly that one could count all of his gold molars. But, grateful or not, his posterior still bubbled out of the side, and the tabletop could not be lowered past his breasts. Out of politeness and defiance both, he remained standing for the whole two-hour session with his back against the wall, shifting from one swollen foot to another and rubbing his back against the cinderblocks like a cat in heat. He never returned, fat deity or not.

When the Vance case had been allotted to him, Judge McCarthy tried everything in his power to get rid of it. He talked to the clerk, to the chief judge, even informally over drinks to the Chief Justice of the Louisiana Supreme Court. In desperation, he even considered a self-recusal, but try as he might to fit a square peg through a round hole, he simply could not meet the statutory conditions. He had to get away from the case because he knew it would be too taxing on him.

That all changed, however, when an old flame called one evening and asked why he had wimped out and not returned to the Buddhism class. "It's a waste of time. I could teach those skinny, pimple-faced brats a thing or two."

She detected the pain in his voice—a pain he had endeavored with varying degrees of success to cover up with bravado and chutzpah throughout his lackluster career—and thought twice about hurling one of her traditional love-insults at him. Instead, Judge Linda Bonaventure, who had just been named to the federal bench and whom Patrick had known and innocently lusted after since their first jobs after law school as assistant district attorneys, convinced him of how integral he was to the process of ensuring that the Louisiana statute under which Vance was being charged—a statute that discriminated between mur-ders caused by secular mutilations on the one hand, and those resulting from ritualistic or religious ones on the other—be rendered a dead letter. He was powerless to oppose her persuasive web-weaving.

To put it simply, he still had the hots for her.

The next day, ostensibly as a consolation prize for Patrick's inability to find a seat into which he could squeeze at Loyola, Judge Bonaventure had a U.S. marshal hand-deliver to his chambers a package containing a pho-tocopy of Judge Hyman's frayed yellow paperback and the Buddha amulet now hanging from his rear-view mirror. On the card accompanying the amulet, she had carefully penned nine words that as yet meant nothing to Judge Patrick McCarthy, but which nonetheless, after nine years of Catholic-school Latin, he was readily able to translate: "*Non trans gentes sed ultra somnia est libertas componenda.*"

✳

"All right, call the next case. And I'm warning y'all now, if there are any outbursts from the audience, I'm gonna have you all carted out in handcuffs on contempt charges. Have I made myself understood?"

The District Attorney smiled nervously and turned around for a second, as if to tell his electorate, "Yea, I know this guy's nuts." Judge McCarthy was truly at home behind the mahogany dais of his courtroom. From his massive leather chair with extendable arms that flapped out every time he sat down, he surveyed the record crowd.

The wood-paneled courtroom, with windows twenty-feet high and oil paintings, four on each side, of the dour jurists who had preceded him at one time or another in Division E of the Orleans Parish Criminal District Court, would have matched any person's preconceived notion of a proper Southern courtroom.

The bailiff lowered his head to a microphone and read out, "Case number 94-134579, State of Louisiana versus Edwin Francis Vance. Counsel, make your appearances for the record, please."

"Donald Faucheux, District Attorney of Orleans Parish, for the State of Louisiana." He wore a brand-new tropical wool suit, charcoal gray with shadowy pinstripes, and a blue Oxford with a red-and-blue paisley tie. He was nearing fifty-five, but with his broad shoulders and solid limbs, he could still pass for a star quarterback. Of course, he had graduated from Jesuit High School; every D.A. for the preceding fifty years had been an alumnus.

"Ira J. Moskowitz, of the Public Defender's office, for the Defendant."

"All right," Judge McCarthy boomed out, "I'd like to have a side-bar with both counsel before we get started." Then, looking at Vance, whose wrists and ankles were shackled together, wearing a bright orange jumper stenciled with the words "Orleans Parish Prison," he added, "Mr. Vance, I just want to assure you that this has nothing to do with your case, it's something personal."

Ed's hair cascaded to the sides over the invisible circumflex that was pointed at the middle of his forehead. Except for the jail attire, he looked as fresh as if he had just completed his nightly primping in front of his office mirror. "I trust you, Your Honor," he answered with a smile.

The judge peered down at the District Attorney and sneered. He covered his microphone. "So, Donald, you actually made it out of bed for this one, huh? And for an arraignment of all things. What's the matter, boy, you couldn't trust such a high-profile case to one of your minions? Or are you taking your orders from somewhere else? City Hall or…no…Baton Rouge, perhaps?" The District Attorney shrugged his shoulders and smiled broadly and contemptuously at his former colleague and nemesis.

How did this fat pig ever manage to get on the bench? How did he ever fit behind it?

Judge McCarthy knew that Donald Faucheux, like most district attorneys in the State of Louisiana, despised him, but he didn't give a shit. Besides, he relished the opportunity to toy with him because the D.A.'s ambition was pure hubris, and the Judge was counting the minutes to his tragic downfall.

"Well, I just want to make myself abundantly clear from the get-go, that I will tolerate no grandstanding of any kind in this case. It's gonna be fair and square all the way through. No dirty tricks come out of the bag in this one, got me?"

Both men nodded their heads and turned back without comment to their respective tables.

The Judge smiled blankly at the audience and said, "Would the Defendant please rise."

Ed stood up, and Judge McCarthy pushed his glasses down his nose and read with deliberation the text of the indictment:

In the Criminal District Court for the Parish of Orleans, on the 8th day of November, 1994, in the matter of the State of Louisiana v. Edwin Francis Vance. The grand jury of the Parish of Orleans charges that said Edwin Francis Vance committed the offense of first-degree murder in that Mr. Vance on the evening of November 1, 1994 killed his wife Stella Carruthers Vance with the specific intent to kill while he was involved in the ritualistic mutilation, dismemberment or torture of Mrs. Vance as part of a ceremony, rite, initiation, observance, performance or practice, in violation of title 14, section 30(A)(7) of the Louisiana Revised Statutes and contrary to the peace and dignity of the State of Louisiana.

Judge McCarthy put the paper down and said, "I'd like the record to reflect that this indictment is an original, has been endorsed a 'true bill' and is signed by the foreman of the grand jury. Would the Defendant like to examine it?"

"No, Your Honor," uttered Ed and his lawyer in unison.

The District Attorney jumped out of his seat and patted down the tailored sides of his new jacket. "Judge, the State has filed this morning a notice of its intent to seek the death penalty in this case."

A hush fell over the room, followed by a soft hum of whispers.

"Trying for a clean sweep, Mr. Faucheux?" The District Attorney of Orleans Parish had sought the death penalty in all twenty-three of his first-degree murder cases the year before, and had succeeded in every one. The press had dubbed him "The Executioner," a title of which he was so proud that he had a nameplate engraved with it and placed on his desk.

"Sir, the crime here was particularly gruesome and…"

"Save it for the jury, Mr. Faucheux. Mr. Vance, has your attorney told you of the State's intention to seek the death penalty?"

"Yes, Sir, he has."

"Good. Then, before you enter a plea, I want to make sure you understand that if you plead not guilty, and a jury of your peers determines beyond a reasonable doubt that you are guilty of the crime of first-degree murder, that same jury may recommend that the death penalty be imposed. Do you understand that?"

"Yes, Your Honor, I do."

"And that if you plead guilty to the charge, this Court cannot sentence you...this Court is prohibited by the Code of Criminal Procedure from imposing the death penalty, and will be compelled to sentence you to a maximum term of life imprisonment without benefit of parole, probation or suspension of sentence. Has your attorney explained that to you as well?"

"Yes, Your Honor, he has."

"Very well. In that case, Mr. Vance, how do you wish to plead to the charge against you?"

"Not guilty, Your Honor."

"Fine, I want all pretrial motions to be filed not more than sixty days from today's date, and we'll hold a hearing on them in...let's see...sometime after Mardi Gras...Bernard, give me a date in March."

"March 17."

"No, that's St. Patrick's Day." The courtroom erupted in laughter, and the District Attorney turned to one of his assistants and rolled his eyes. Professor Hardwick, sitting in the far right corner of the back row, started to cough uncontrollably. "Let's say March 20, 1995. Mr. Vance, is that acceptable?"

"Yes, Your Honor, that's fine."

The District Attorney stood up and fidgeted with his tie for a moment too long. The judge interrupted him: "Gotta look pretty for that camera, ain't that right, Mr. Faucheux?"

He would ignore the slight, but his crimson cheeks betrayed his embarrassment. "Your Honor, the State respectfully requests that you set a trial date as well, and we object to giving this Defendant sixty days to file pretrial motions. We have a con…"

Judge McCarthy's eyes bulged out as he slammed his fists down on the desk, his fleshy cheeks and nose lividly purple. "Mr. District Attorney, one more outburst like that, one more pathetic attempt to get your friends at the newspapers to taint the jury pool, and I will hold you in contempt and entertain a motion by the Defendant right here in open court to transfer the venue of this trial to Calcasieu Parish."

"I'm sorry, Your Honor."

"Now, as for setting a trial date, I don't want to prejudge the merits of Mr. Vance's pretrial motions without seeing them. It would be…I don't know…bad karma." The courtroom rumbled again.

"Mr. Faucheux, the State's objection is duly noted and overruled. As they should have taught you in law school, the trial on a capital felony must by statute begin no later than three years after the initiation of proceedings. This is intended to protect whom? The State? No, you would be happy as a pig in mud to keep these trials going as long as possible because the accused is incarcerated prior to and during trial. So, who? Every civics student in any decent high school—even Jesuit, I assume—could guess that this is for the benefit of the Defendant. Likewise, the constitutional right to a speedy trial is designed to protect the Defendant, not the State, and this Defendant," the judge pointed to Mr. Vance, "this Defendant, Mr. Vance, has said that sixty days is fine with him. Isn't that right, Mr. Vance, or would you prefer me to set pretrial motions for two weeks or a month from now?"

"No, Sir, sixty days is fine. I believe my lawyer will appreciate the extra time."

The public defender bowed his head in shame and gratitude. He was sloppy and slovenly, and his slicked-back hair needed washing. A threadbare blue linen suit draped limply from his muscleless shoulders and his rubber-soled shoes were badly scoffed from parking-lot gravel. While the District Attorney sipped Sazeracs every night with his bevy of politicos at Ruth's Chris on Broad and Orleans, he was burning the midnight oil in his cubicle wading through four-foot stacks of manila folders, all for eighteen thousand seven hundred dollars a year.

"Very well. Thank you, gentlemen. And Mr. Moskowitz, if you find you need more time for those pretrial motions, I will certainly entertain a motion for extension of time at the appropriate juncture. OK?" He peered down over his reading glasses at the District Attorney, who was now heaving with anger. "The State has opted to pursue the death penalty, so y'all down at South White have chosen to make this a question of life and death. Ergo, like it or not, the State's just gonna have to live with the judicial process going along at a pace commensurate with the magnitude of the issue involved." He slowly brought his coffee mug to his mouth and sipped the now cold liquid. "The expedited track is for landlords seeking back-paid rent, not for persons accused of first-degree murder and facing death by lethal injection." One could have heard a pin drop. "Understood?"

Only the Defendant's table budged.

"Good, I thought so. Have a nice day, counselors. Good day, Mr. Vance. Call the next case, please…"

Three

Three times a week—Mondays, Wednesdays and Saturdays—at a lopsided dive on the corner of Iberville and Burgundy, Professor Dylan Hardwick held court. Rarely were there more than two or three supplicants before him, but the one appearing on this particular night—Andrew Sear—never failed to appear. This suited Professor Hardwick just fine because from his barstool he would dispense judgments, maledictions, and sometimes even advice, whether Andy was listening or even present, for in point of fact, it was to Andy, and Andy alone, that Professor Hardwick would direct his soliloquies. He considered all other law students "fucking embarrassments" and, in his own inimitable way, the childless Professor Hardwick had begun to view Andy not as a friend (for that would imply equality), but as his heir apparent to the throne of snappy retorts.

Andy didn't much care for the Kitty Kat Korner, which did not match the preconceived notion that Andy had of an authentic French Quarter drinking hole, much less of an oak-paneled courtroom, when he arrived from New York three years earlier. He was always amused, and often intrigued, by the sparse but motley crew of New Orleans night people who floated through the joint on any given night: teenaged boy hustlers, lunatics, ex-cops in leather, and priests in civilian garb, to name but a few. Cheap drinks flowed, pot billowed away, and neither the bartenders nor the police ever asked any questions.

"What a filthy afterthought this place is…that's just what it is, Dylan, an *afterthought*."

Professor Hardwick was already working on his fourth Sazerac of the evening's session, or in his own words, "just warming up." "Afterthought's being a bit charitable, wouldn't you say?" He drank down to the halfway mark, started sucking an ice-cube and shouted, "Fucking lousy service too, if you ask me."

Bruno the bartender shot him the finger, and Professor Hardwick raised his plastic cup to return the toast. Even though the drinks were only $1.75 a piece, the Korner offered its other patrons real glasses, but the professor, perennially afraid that he might catch some deadly germ left behind by a fellow wanderer, insisted on drinking from sterile plastic as long as it was the sixteen-ounce opaque kind.

Dylan and Andy had gone through a lot together in the previous three years, and Andy sometimes wondered how he ever would have survived law school with his sanity intact had he never met Dylan. They were kindred souls in so many ways: Both had few friends, and even fewer *real* ones, and their friendship, which, beyond all the banter, was founded on respect, admiration and just a smidgen of mutual envy, was truly and healthily symbiotic.

Being a Wednesday, November 1st fell on one of their regularly scheduled nights out at the Korner, but tonight the dynamic duo would certainly be out until dawn because Andy had to be prepped—"mentally and *spiritually*," Dylan had said—for the most important interview of his life.

As always, Professor Hardwick was scrambling hopelessly to hop back onto the outskirts of a tangent, which meant that he was bound, sooner rather than later, to repeat "The Rules" for the thousandth time. Rolling his eyes, Andy was not disappointed:

"For God's sake, Andy, what's the first fucking thing I taught you? Don't you remember? It's *all* buried in the footnotes. All of it: history, religion, law, genealogy, you name it. If you really wanna know what the truth is, just read the goddamned footnotes!"

Professor Dylan Hardwick was devoted, as much as he could be, to the Truth with a capital T, but he rarely used the word anymore. He said he was becoming "jaded."

"No, you're just stuck in your own little echo chamber," Andy countered.

"Not quite accurate, my dear fellow, for I'm stuck in a *lush* little echo chamber. In fact, come to think of it, I'm a lush *in* a little echo chamber. Ha ha ha…what d'ya know? I made a funny. Write that down, Andy, 'cause that's what I want you to put on my tombstone before the fucking Jesuits get to me."

Professor Dylan Hardwick had no intention of ever being buried even in the vicinity of a Catholic cemetery, much less administered the Rite of Anointing the Sick by a Jesuit priest, and Andy knew as much. A self-proclaimed, albeit false, atheist in a Catholic law school, Dylan had many flaws, but one generally recognized and as yet unchallenged claim to fame: Six years before, he had risked being denied tenure forever by daring to remove the crucifix suspended above his blackboard. As a result, he found *himself* suspended for a week, and after the fall (so to speak), he found himself hopscotching endlessly in the chasm between voluptuary manqué and eccentric enigma. There remained in his face and his demeanor the remnants of a relatively attractive man, but he camouflaged them well by dressing as if he were still a college sophomore roaming around Greenwich Village: faded Levi's bubbling across his ever-bloated midsection, a T-shirt bearing some cryptic or offensive slogan, and pock-marked sandals. Despite many pretensions of scholarship, he never wrote so much as a law review article, an endeavor that he equated with "masturbating in a mirror." Instead, he took full advantage of his abundant free time by seeking out new opportunities to cheat on his dowdy wife with female law students and to rummage through the underbrush in Audubon Park for a spot in the shade where he could flip off his sandals and drink his Jim Beam from a brown paper bag.

To Andy, depending on the topic under attack, Dylan could be a blowhard, a tragic hero, an addict in denial or a moral reprobate—sometimes even all four at the same time. Their sessions together were never boring, but they were often embarrassing and invariably exhausting mentally. Because of the huge quantity of alcohol typically consumed in the course of one, they were beginning to take their physical toll on Andy as well. He occasionally experienced lightning flashes of doubt, when he thought it would be best for his career, not to mention his sanity, if he stopped socializing (which meant *drinking*) with Dylan once and for all. But, in the end, he weathered them all, for something about Dylan's heterodoxy beckoned Andy in a way that nothing before in his life had.

Andy glanced at his Timex nervously. "So, Dylan, how much longer are we going to ignore the pink elephant in the corner?"

The professor snapped out of a daze. "Ha?…what?…Oh, that…Yeah, well, I guess we can't let this whole damned evening go to pot. Hey, speaking of pot, why don't you roll the next one. I'll order a refill. Hey, Bruno…"

"You're avoiding the issue…"

"No, I'm not, Andy, I just need a little brain fuel. Preparing for an interview with Judge Santa isn't a fucking picnic in the sun."

Bruno, a solid, bald-headed biker with an uncanny resemblance to Mr. Clean, poured a more than generous double shot of bourbon into Andy's glass, then dragged the bottle over to Professor Hardwick's hollow cup.

"Why don't you give this kid's ears a break, man?"

"And why don't you go fuck yourself," Dylan barked. Bruno smirked as he walked away.

"Getting back to the pink elephant…"

"Look, Andy, don't blame me if your fucking legal career is going down the drain. That's all your own goddamned fault, buddy."

Andy had to open his mouth before the wound set in. "Now you sound like my mother."

This was absolutely true, and it pierced Dylan to the core. He had never had children precisely because he never wanted to be accused of being anyone's parent.

"Andy, you remember the Trump Rule?"

Oh shit, here we go again.

"Would you like me to recite it, Professor, or will you do the honors?"

"I like hearing my ageless wisdom emanating gently from your lips, so please be my guest."

Andy stared down at his drink and facetiously droned: "Just tell me who has to win the case and I'll write the facts accordingly. People, wake up for Christ's sake, cases are not won on the merits…"

Professor Hardwick jumped up from his stool and nearly tumbled to the ground. "Sorry, it's my low blood pressure…Yes, Andy, 'they're won on the bloody facts. Facts always trump. All hail to the facts!'" Both men raised their chins and saluted the mirror over the booze bottles.

"You know, Dylan, I've been thinking about that rule lately, and it seems to me that the so-called 'Trump Rule' might actually infringe on a certain business magnate's proprietary rights."

Like a genius who has just been bested by an undergraduate, Dylan shoved his middle finger into Andy's face as he shook his head in pity: "Boy, it really is time you went out and got laid…and, hey, why wait? We can hook you up with the little blond surfer boy at the end of the bar to give you a quickie in the bathroom stall. A desperate situation calls for desperate measures, right? What's a blowjob now, Bruno…about forty bucks?"

The bartender ignored him, but Andy was getting perturbed by his professor's dancing around the issue at hand: "Hard-dee-har-har…thou slayest me. Did you stay up all night thinking that one up?"

"Hardly, Andy my boy. I have millions more where that came from…"

Andy had to bring the banter to a close. "I bet. So, Dylan, let's get back…"

"Not so fast, cowboy. You may be beyond help at this point. You lost your chance last year."

Andy knew immediately the incident to which Professor Hardwick was referring. The wound was still fresh. Teacher and student, true to form, had been drinking in the Kitty Kat Korner that night, on the same barstools, to celebrate Andy's class rank: first in common law, and fourth in the combined common- and civil-law curricula. Professor Hardwick, though, hated celebrations as a general principle and simply had to dilute Andy's mirth with a rude awakening to the facts.

"Andy, listen to me for once in your life. You never got the editor-in-chief spot on the fucking law review. Instead, you let those good-for-nothing dykes slam dunk you. Without that, no matter whose dick I suck to get you a job, you can kiss goodbye to a clerkship with a federal judge, even one as fucked up as Jonas Santa Claus Hyman, and without that your future in the Supreme Court goes flying out the Emerald fucking City and over the rainbow." As he waved farewell to Andy's career, Bruno trotted over. "Hey, ass-wipe, another round for me and my friend who's off to Oz. That's right, Andy, you better pucker up and start kissing some Munchkin ass, or start leavin' on a jet plane back to harvesting tea leaves or whatever the fuck you did during the year you were fucking off in Paraguay."

Professor Hardwick saw that his protege was hurt, and as a way of retreating, snatching up Andy's fresh glass of bourbon. "Bruno, shake your ass and splash some Pernod and bitters in this drink for my partner." Then, pushing the glass across the mahogany, he exclaimed, "For Christ's sake, Andy, you're in New Orleans. Have a Sazerac and drink the fuck up…."

*

Andy knew instinctively that Dylan was right—no law school graduate from a third-rate law school like Loyola gets to the Supreme Court without passing through a federal district judge, perhaps even a federal appellate judge or two beforehand, and the federal judges won't see you unless you were editor-in-chief of your law review—but not getting the position was definitely not his fault. As the rumor went, someone on the previous year's editorial board had been "put off" by Andrew Sear—a recurrent theme in Andy's life, but one to which he slowly but surely had become accustomed. He had assumed that the board couldn't deny him *some* position, because he *was*, after all, at the top of his class, and, on that point, he had been right. Thus, when the outgoing triumvirate had asked Andy whether he would be willing take one of the two managing editor spots, he immediately conceded, although he had had absolutely no interest in verifying case citations and scouring the fonts used in the thousands of meaningless footnotes that no ordinary person ever bothered to read anyway.

Andy had reconciled himself the previous year to his fate, but only halfheartedly, and it only took a few words from his trusted mentor over too many Sazeracs to rip away the scab. Dylan felt bad for "the kid," as he called him behind his back, but he explained the decision to Andy as logically as possible: "It was a fucking political decision...those gutless cocksuckers...I knew it. They had to stack the board with niggers and dykes...they got pushed into a fucking corner by the alumni fundraisers, fucking pussies. Well, no easy way to put it, Andy, you got screwed. So, spread your legs wide and drink the fuck up!"

✳

Andy struggled to divert the sting of blaming himself once again for his strategic flops. "Those who forget the past are condemned to repeat it," murmured Andy.

"George Santayana...so you do know something after all, huh? Well, whaddya wanna know, my boy? Let me enlighten you so you can go home and get your beauty sleep. After all, you gotta have your smiley face on tomorrow for Santa, even though it's a fucking waste of time."

The interview with Judge Hyman...what am I gonna do about this fucking interview? Dylan's three sheets to the wind, it's coming up on four o'clock in the morning, and I still don't know what I have to do to clinch this fucking clerkship.

Andy was panicking because no matter what, he still harbored the dream of being a law clerk to a Supreme Court Justice, and editor-or-chief or not, he was the top of his class and was determined to get a federal clerkship. Professor Dylan Hardwick—the antiestablishment guru, the malcontent, the drunk—was his ticket into The Honorable Judge Jonas Hyman's chambers at the Eastern District of Louisiana. Dylan Hardwick, way back in the old days of sobriety and unbridled intelligence, had worked as an associate in Hyman's firm, and despite their disagreements in the years since Hyman fired Dylan and rose to the federal bench, Judge Hyman still regarded Dylan as a son, even if a wayward one. All that it would take, Andy was convinced, was a word of recommendation from Dylan to his former boss now become federal judge, named by the President of the United States to a term that ended only upon the judge's death.

Andy's mind was doing somersaults. Despite his desperation and intoxication, Andy needed to avoid a collision with Dylan, who never had taken kindly to his lofty aspirations, and was raring to go for at least another few rounds. Dylan beat Andy to the punch: "OK, buddy, I see it in your eyes again, but forget about it. Just forget about it. You're never going to Washington with a degree from this fucking dump, even if it's *summa cum laude*, you can be sure of that, my friend!" So, Andy tried to sneak in through the back door.

"Dylan, remember that letter I got from Justice Souter?"

"Sure do," Dylan answered, neither looking up nor taking his drink away from his mouth. "You got some fucking *cojones*, I'll give you that much."

❋

Two and a half years back, at the end of his first semester in law school, Andy had found himself suffocating in the boredom of introductory classes and the monotony of obscenely stupid questions posed by obscenely ignorant classmates clamoring for the dubious distinction of catching their professor's attention. He sought fresh air in the only

place that was still his—his dreams—and hopped again
onto the letter-writing path. Because Professor Hardwick
had instilled in him a real love for constitutional law, he decided to write to all the sitting justices on the United States
Supreme Court, seeking their advice on how to become
a federal judge (in the first draft of the letters, he actually wrote "Supreme Court justice" but, after concluding
that such an ambition might sound a bit too presumptuous coming from a first-year law student, he descended to
a less rarefied altitude).

Seven never answered, but responses from the remaining two came within days. The prize went to Andy's hero,
Harry A. Blackmun, author of *Roe v. Wade* who had been
Nixon's third choice to fill the seat vacated by Abe Fortas.
He had written Andy: "Justice Tom Clark in a speech
once said that 'you have to be on the corner when the bus
comes by.' Fortuitous circumstances must arrive." Without any conscious inkling of the future that awaited him,
Andy promptly framed this letter and hung it over his desk,
but it was only years later, while having to read and reread
the text and footnotes of the Revelation of Anakum, that
the full weight of its layers of meaning hit him.

✳

Justice David Souter had also given Andy a refreshingly
frank word of advice, and as Andy was trying just before
dawn on the day of his interview to resign himself to the
fact that he might not get the job with Judge Jonas Hyman
of the District Court for the Eastern District of Louisiana,
he repeated that advice from memory: "'*I pretty much agree*

with Euripides and Justice Holmes that things tend not to turn out as expected and planning one's life is a waste of time.' You remember that, Dylan? Maybe I should just resign myself to whatever will be."

Professor Hardwick was pointing to the bottle of Wild Turkey when he exploded: "Jesus H. Christ...thanks a lot, Andy boy...A pat dismissal from someone who has reached his plateau to someone who will never even get to the base of the mountain. Don't you see the subtext in there, the pompous gloating cloaked in a cheap rag of erudition?"

Andy, frightened of not getting a clerkship with Judge Hyman, was scalded by his mentor's criticism which, he knew, was actually aimed at him rather than Justice Souter. Fueled by booze and pot, he could not hold his tongue: "Hold on for a second, Dylan, 'cause you're totally off base. Only an idiot wouldn't see the brilliance and honesty of this statement."

Professor Hardwick lit up like a Christmas tree and closed his eyes to focus. "Wait a minute, Andy, say that again."

"What? The stuff about Euripides?"

"No, numb nuts, I heard that. What did you just say to me?"

Andy backed off. "Look, Dylan, I'm not calling you an..."

"No, no, that's it...exactly. Tell me *exactly* what you said."

Andy was beginning to get somewhat concerned that Dylan would really slam him now (after all, he was a drunk), so he aimed at sounding defensive and apologetic in the same breath: "Dylan, what I said, and I didn't mean anything by it…I mean, for Christ's sake, I owe you everything I've learned…"

"Oh, shove that shit back up your ass where it's coming from before your brains leak out. This is important. Repeat what you fucking said."

Andy resigned himself to his fate. "What I said was that only an idiot wouldn't see the brilliance of that statement."

"Exactly." Professor Hardwick jumped up from his chair and started waving his hands out. "Bruno, just bring the fucking bottle over here and leave it. You think I'm gonna stiff you?" Then, grabbing Andy by the shoulders and shaking him, he whispered: "My dear Andy, you have the eyes of a cynic, but the heart of a pope. My God. Don't you see you've been assessing the meaning of this statement from the wrong angle?"

Andy was lost, or so he thought, so he kept his tongue. "Which statement? Souter's?"

Dylan, though nodding, was tripping on the chain of thoughts that came pouring out of his mouth. "Just hear me out, Andy. Our dear Mr. Justice Souter wrote that planning one's life is a waste of time because it doesn't turn out as expected. And you said only an idiot wouldn't see the brilliance of that statement. Right?"

Andy nodded.

"So, if our discussion here tonight were being written down…"

Andy was beginning to see the locomotive coming out of the tunnel. "Like in a court opinion, or transcribed in a deposition…"

"Exactly…then any two-bit lawyer doing a search would pull up these two phrases on Lexus and deduce, quite logically, that Andrew Sear believes that Justice Souter is brilliant, and so brilliant, in fact, that only an idiot wouldn't see his brilliance."

"Problem is…" The lights in the bar shot on for dawn had arrived, concomitantly with the switch flicking on in Andy's brain.

"Right, Andy, right…problem is…oh my God, this is positively colossal…problem is that the intermediate step is missing, because in point of fact, my friend, that wasn't your meaning at all. No, you were actually responding to *my* comment about the words being a thirty-two-cent cop-out. I knocked you down a few pegs, and you had to get even. So, the meaning of your statement that Souter's comment is brilliant was not that Souter was brilliant; it was actually that I, the honorable Professor Dylan Hardwick, Ph.D., am a pompous, balloon-bursting prick, an envious fucking idiot whose advice is not to be trusted… and you, Andy Sear…why, you're the brilliant one."

The lights grew dimmer. Andy was getting confused in the tangle of logical deductions amid the haze of pot smoke. He took the easy way out and threw up his hands. "I confess…I guess you outed me."

"Yeah, I know, but Andy, do you realize the *implications* of this? You have overturned the foundations of two centuries of *stare decisis* in one fell swoop because the way in which we stupid aping lawyers are taught to do legal research is fundamentally flawed and unreliable."

"Yeah, I see what you mean…I think."

Professor Hardwick started tracing in the air as if he were writing with chalk on his blackboard. "This, my friend, is a new rule…let's see…how's this: 'When interpreting the true meaning of a court's opinion, you *must* as a threshold matter identify *whom* the court is intending to address and…and…'"

"'…and fill in the gaps.' How's that?"

"Now that's what I call true legal reasoning. Sounds like we've found ourselves another rule, Andy. What shall we call it?"

Andy was happy to take credit for his discovery, but he was still unsure how, or indeed whether, he had stumbled upon it. "How about the Souter Rule?"

"No, no, no…absolutely not. This is definitely not a time for modesty. No, sir, this is henceforth to be known throughout the realm as the Andrew Sear Rule."

"Whatever you say, Dylan."

Professor Hardwick, as woozy from the mixture of booze and pot as from the liberating exhilaration of this find, poured both of them another shot of Wild Turkey, passed the joint over to Andy, and said "I hereby christen thee the Andrew Sear Rule. Congratulations, young man, you have now entered eternity."

❋

"Now, can we get back to Judge Hyman? Please! I mean, Dylan, I don't understand why you couldn't just call the guy and tell him to hire me. Why do I have to go through all this rigmarole?"

"Oh, stop whining. And anyway, be careful what you wish for. Like I said, he's no fucking picnic to be around."

Andy was getting distressed because Dylan had now said this twice. "And what exactly do you mean by that?"

"Jonas Hyman is like a fucking stale Twinkie: soft and mushy on the outside, hard and clotted on the inside."

Andy gulped. "So, he's a prick to work for? I mean, are you setting me up for a fall?"

"Paranoid tonight, Magellan, aren't we? What I mean is that he's a bit over-the-top sometimes."

"And coming from one as straight-laced as you, that means what?"

"Ha ha…yeah…but don't laugh, he's a kooky old bird. Him and that bitch-on-wheels of a St. Bernard twat he's always hanging around with."

"Who?"

"Ah…so you aren't up to date on courthouse scandals…Linda Bonaventure. The word is that he's been fucking her, but personally, I doubt it. I mean Hyman's married to a real looker…you know her, I'm sure…Victoria Hyman, the newscaster?"

"Sure, I heard that."

"Besides I think Hyman's a eunuch. In any case, Linda Bonaventure doesn't quite match up. She's nothing but a bleached-blond wannabe dyke from way over the parish line who loves criminals. She even shakes their hands when they come into her courtroom. You may meet her, 'cause she's always in chambers at night drinking with Jonas."

"Sounds like an interesting pair…"

"They're not. He's got…I mean, they've got…some pretty rigid beliefs too, and he's really into all of this life-affirming, self-help, I'm-OK-you're-OK bullshit. If you really want to get on his good side quick, don't waste your time talking about law review because he thinks it's as much of a circle jerk as I do. No, if you want to win over this man, just volunteer all sorts of personal dilemmas…you know, family shit, intimacy problems…I mean, tell him you've been in New Orleans for three fucking years and still can't get laid…he eats that crap up."

"You mean, just start blurting out stuff at random?"

"No…it can't be just any old scoop…it's gotta be something juicy or bordering on scandalous…I'm convinced the old bastard gets off on the shit." He downed half his drink. "Ah, yeah, and don't forget that he's far too polite and circumspect to ask you any such sensitive questions, so don't wait for any cues. Grin through a couple of minutes of the obligatory small talk, which he hates anyway, and just start venting…I mean, don't hold back…regurgitate it right out in front of him, like you're seeking some grandfatherly advice, and I guarantee he'll love you forever." After refilling his cup, Dylan turned away from looking at his friend and murmured into his drink: "He'll probably wind up worshipping the ground you walk on. After all, he needs somebody to take my place."

Andy knew that Dylan was screaming out for his bruised ego to be massaged, but he was growing a little impatient with his mentor's self-pity. "So, no talk about the law, huh?"

"Not a peep," answered Dylan as he slurped the last few drops of his sixth Sazerac and belched loudly. "But, you might try raising the subject of Ed Vance, the insurance god who bust open his wife's skull in some sort of fucking weird religious ritual." Andy looked at him quizzically.

"What? The great Andrew Sear, Supreme Court wannabe, didn't read about the case that's going to make or break law?"

"Yeah, I did. Strange." Andy had nearly memorized the reports in the paper about the murder. *A ritualistic murder, right here in New Orleans.*

Professor Hardwick inhaled what little bourbon remained in the cracks in the ice at the bottom of his plastic cup. "Yeah, in fact, that case has been assigned to McCarthy down at CDC, and Hyman and McCarthy go way back. They belong to the same Mardi Gras krewe and they are always getting together to shoot the shit."

As the first rays of sunlight peered in through the window, Andy could not follow where Dylan's trail was leading. "And?"

"Are you brain dead, Andy? You wanna get a job with Santa Claus, you gotta bring a gift. Tell Hyman to get you hooked up working on that Vance case. I'm sure the public defender they got on it wouldn't know how to argue himself out of a plastic bag."

Andy knew much more black-letter law than Professor Dylan Hardwick, whose instincts as a litigator were flawless, even at those all-too-frequent times when his senses were impaired by drugs and alcohol. "Dylan, be serious. I just got out of law school. You need to be a member of the Bar for five years before you can be assigned to a capital murder case."

"Bruno, get me another fucking drink." The bartender glared back as Dylan looked sheepishly into his wounded protege's eyes. "Well, I'm still a member of the Bar, at least last time I looked. You can put my name down as lead counsel and we'll work on it together...I mean, with you doing all the work and me getting all the glory."

Instead of telling Dylan to fuck off, Andy got a glimmer in his eyes. "So, you mean take the case over from the public defender."

Dylan crunched up his mouth, and for a moment, Andy thought his former teacher might have to vomit. "You jerk-off, this is Orleans Parish, remember? The guy's gonna be convicted and sentenced to death. We'll take over the appeals and post-conviction stuff because the public defender can't."

Four

Andy nodded at the guard, who with a look of revulsion removed the handcuffs.

"If you get any trouble, Mr. Sear, just call out; I'm just on the other side of the door."

Andy ignored the guard. "And remove the ankle chains, too."

"I need to get approval from the warden for that, Sir."

"Just do what I say. I'm his lawyer and I'm not going to sit here while he's shackled." Andy surprised even himself with his resolve. The guard, shaking his head, snapped open the chains and left the room with them dangling at his side.

Ed was smiling at his lawyer. "Thanks for that. You're the first person I've met since being here who's treated me like a human being."

"You're welcome, Ed." Andy's heart was still beating fast from standing up to the guard.

Just then, the door creaked and swung open again, and the guard reappeared. Andy had given him four quarters, and he brought back a couple of Barq's root beers, which he dutifully poured into plastic cups. This was no sign of genteel Southern hospitality, but merely blind compliance with the warden's orders: after all, the sharp edges of the pull-tab of an aluminum can might conceivably be used as a dangerous weapon.

Cradling the cup in his freed hands, Ed sipped the cold drink as if it were the rarest cognac. Then he smiled again at Andy, not a reluctant smile, but this time a broad display of his deep dimples. His teeth were perfectly straight and well tended. At first glance, one might even have concluded that he was guilty of the mortal sin of vanity were it not for the fact that he was sitting on Death Row in the middle of nowhere because he had killed his wife in cold blood.

"I really appreciate what you did for me, getting the stay and all. I heard that it cost you your job. Just know that I'm grateful to you forever." He continued sipping the root beer and looking into Andy's eyes. His chin was square, his nose aquiline, and every feature of his body so delicate and sculpted that many people had found him effeminate and drawn their own conclusions about him. "So, you have a J.D., right?"

"Yes, I do." Andy had no idea where this was going and started to feel a bit antsy.

"And that means *juris doctor*, doctor of law, right?"

"Yes. But, it's only a title, and I seem to recall some philosopher saying that titles are life's greatest deception because the only way you can get rid of them is by killing everyone around you." As he spoke the lines, he realized what a stupid, inappropriate witticism it had been.

"Well, maybe the philosopher is you. You definitely remind me of a philosopher." Ed took a swig of his root beer but didn't move his eyes. Andy, though, still felt uncomfortable, thinking that, perhaps, Ed might leap out of his seat at any moment and strangle him to death. "So, I think I should call you Dr. Sear, not Andy. After all, you're a doctor."

"I seem to remember that the state bar association issued an advisory opinion a few years back that lawyers should refrain from calling themselves doctors."

"Well, that doesn't make any sense...your degree says *juris doctor*, so you're a doctor. Maybe the AMA got upset because of the competition." He winked. "So, that settles it. Agreed, Doctor?" Ed reached across the table and patted Andy on the shoulder. Maybe Andy was imagining it, but Ed actually beamed at him, and bobbed his head up and down like a lanky teenager who had been kissed for the first time. From that moment on, Andy always saw him in that pose, in that moment: a hybrid of Ben Affleck's chin and eyes, Colin Farrell's body, and the mischievous smile of some heartthrob from the Mexican *telenovelas* whose name Andy unfortunately couldn't remember.

How could my Calvin Klein poster boy be facing execution for the crime of first-degree murder?

From that first interview forward, all of the letters and poems that Ed Vance sent to him were addressed to Dr. Andy Sear, Esq. in care of the Kit Kat Realty Co. on Poydras Street.

The guard interrupted the two of them.

Andy leapt out of his seat, so precipitously that he surprised even himself. "What do you want? Do I need to call the warden?"

"Sir, I'm sorry...I was just wantin' to ask if y'all wanted to eat some lunch. The warden says I can bring it in to y'all in here."

Andy didn't feel much like eating lunch. He had stopped for a good old-fashioned country breakfast just outside of Baton Rouge because he knew he could never get by on jail fare after a three-hour drive from New Orleans. Halfway through the thought, two Styrofoam trays—each overflowing with three pieces of fried chicken and a catcher's mitt of mashed potatoes and gravy, topped with steaming rolls and a couple of brownies— were dropped in the middle of the desk. Some of the gravy dripped onto Andy's pants.

"I know all this starch ain't too good for your pretty little figure, Ed, but I'm sure you'll make do just fine. And Mr. Sear, plastic spoons only. Warden's orders…"

Ed ignored the insult, but wasted no time in retaliating: "Sir, you should really call him *Dr.* Sear, not *Mr.* Sear. I'm sure your mother taught you to respect education."

He looked baffled. "I thought he was a lawyer. What you doin' with your own private physician in here? Does the warden know about this?"

"Relax," Andy interrupted. "I have a doctorate in law, so people call me Dr."

"Jesus Christ, you done nearly gave me a heart attack."

Ed and Andy laughed and started eating. "You know, Dr. Sear, the guard's not a bad sort, and he's right in a certain way. They're trying to overdose us on carbohydrates…never any green salads or nuts…just starch, starch, and more starch. I've put on twenty pounds since I've been here."

Andy wished that twenty extra pounds looked as good on himself. A million retorts shot into his mind, but he was not yet at the stage in his relationship where he could be honestly self-deprecating. Nor did he feel entirely comfortable broaching the only question that was prickling him: not how Ed kept his skin so smooth, or whether he missed his wife, or who was bringing snow cones to his kids now that summer was going full blast. Andy felt like a school kid again.

"Ed, if you don't mind me asking…and you don't have to answer me if you don't want to…but…aren't you afraid of being sodomized?"

He grinned and swallowed. "Well, Dr. Sear, the truth is that solitary confinement does have its advantages." He winked and they both started laughing.

They spent about six hours together. The air conditioner failed after lunch, and though sweat poured down his forehead, matting his undershirt to his skin, Andy didn't want to leave. At one point, Ed grabbed his napkin and without getting off his chair, patted Andy's brow dry.

"Dr. Sear, they're doing this on purpose, you know, burning you out. They wanna get rid of you because you've been here too long."

"Ed, I'd really appreciate it if you'd just call me Andy. When I hear Dr. Sear, I keep thinking my father is looking over my shoulder."

"Sure thing, Andy."

Ed told Andy about his wife Stella, his three children Sammy, Jonathan and Rachel, and his girlfriend Josephine. He worried constantly about his parents, and though his in-laws had been awarded permanent custody of his children, he had absolutely nothing but good things to say about them. Of course, he cried a few times, but overall he seemed to be in no great distress at all. He was at peace with himself.

"Andy, what religion are you, if you don't mind me asking?"

"Well, Ed, that's not an easy question. I guess I'm Catholic, but I really don't know. I have a graduate degree in theology, and I thought that would help me define myself, but I guess I'm still searching."

"Sounds familiar." He looked right at Andy, still smiling, and asked without any hint of a non sequitur: "Andy, have you ever heard of Anakum?"

"Not really…well, wait a minute. I remember reading in one of the news magazines about a political group in the Middle East that was being tortured. I think they were called the Anakumists. Anyway, I'm not sure. So, what is it?"

"Well, it's a he, and he changed my life. You need to read his Revelation."

"Fact or fiction?"

"No, fact. Definitely fact. You'll never be the same after you read it. I'll ask my mother-in-law to send it to you."

"Sure, I'll be happy to."

When the time finally came for Andy to leave because the mosquitoes were targeting him like Scud missiles, Ed hugged him tightly, and just as Andy was letting go, kissed his neck. As a reflex, Andy grabbed him by the cheeks with the palms of his hands, then wiped aside Ed's tears with his index fingers. He had the innocence—maybe that's the wrong word—the *purity*—of a child, and Andy confessed that he was beginning to feel emotions for Ed that he had not felt in a long time for anyone.

"God be with you." Andy turned away because he was afraid to keep looking into Ed's eyes.

"Read the book, Andy. Please don't forget to read it."

Part Two

THE REVELATION OF ANAKUM

THE REVELATION OF ANAKUM

Testimony of the Prophet

I swear by the power, and in the name, of Tupã, who is Father, Son and Holy Spirit, Allah, the Eternal One, the Unutterable, that the testimony I am about to give is true and accurate.

I am a man who was baptized into the Roman Catholic Church through no choice of my own. I have always harbored a belief in God, but I have never dedicated much thought to it, although in my dreams it is evident that I have sought Him out and listened to Him and been led by Him.

My name is unimportant. I am only a man. I could be anyone, and the fact that it is I who am writing this in the year 1984 is merely serendipitous.

I was confirmed into the Roman Catholic Church. It has been thirty-six years since my last confession. I have received none of the other Sacraments.

By profession, I am a merchant of moderate success, but I began my working life as a volunteer teacher of English as a Second Language in Paraguay.

On Friday, August 3, 1984, I entered the Hotel Gloria on

Calle Potosí in La Paz, Bolivia. I asked for a room that faced Illimani. It was cold. My toes were trembling. I could not warm up. I sat at the desk and looked out at Illimani as the sun reached its zenith. I began to chew coca and drink water, and words streamed into my mind. They flowed like a river, smoothly and purely. They were words I had never heard or read before, but they did not seem foreign.

For the next six days, I transcribed the stream of words that came into my mind. I had no other activity in La Paz except to go out every day to buy coca and bicarbonate of soda from the *cholita* on the corner of Illampu and Santa Cruz and to have lunch and a *chuflay* at Pizzería Eli on the Prado.

The entire text of the words that I channeled is contained within the booklet entitled *The Revelation of Anakum*. Not a single syllable has been omitted or substituted. Some words were communicated in English, others in Spanish, others in Guaraní. I transcribed them exactly as my mind dictated them to me, and did not try to interpret them.

I give praise to Tupã, the Unutterable, for allowing an ordinary man without a name to be the channel through which his latest revelation came to a world in political turmoil and spiritual inertia.

The revelation that follows does not replace or supersede any other revelation from heaven. The prophets and messengers of the past, just like the saints, always have their place, and this place can never be supplanted. The Unutterable does not err in communicating his word, but as the Master of All, retains the privilege and discretion to speak as He wishes when He wishes depending on the circumstances. The circumstances are dire, and they will worsen over the next fifty years. The entire world order as we know it today will cease to exist. It is up to us to listen and act accordingly.

I wrote this testimony in my own hand in La Paz, Bolivia on the 10th day of August, 1984, but did not sign it because I am a man without a name, responding to the imperative of the Unutterable.

---

[1] "I sleep" in Guaraní. The titles occur in all of the five extant manuscripts as the first word of the paragraph, not as a separate caption, following a tradition seen in the first five books of Moses (e.g., the Hebrew word for Genesis, *bereshith*, is not a title, but

Akê[1]

When the hair over my ears was turning from black to white, I left the cradle of the mountains where I had always lived to walk to the place where the sun slept. By our way of counting, I had created five children, but in the Jungle of the Karaí,[2] I learned a different way of counting, and found out that I had created seventeen. All except one boy had died or been corrected.

On the day that I left, only my father, my son, and a member of the goldsmith clan remained alive in Chuguiagu. All the other stone houses ringing the inside of the great crater had been empty since the previous winter. As soon as the goldsmith replaced me as *tuvicha*,[3] I left to find a woman so that the rules could always be followed and so that

---

merely the first word of the book). They have thus become proper nouns, much like Genesis and Deuteronomy in the Old Testament.

[2]Karaí is not a proper name, but the Guaraní word for "gentleman." In the first German translation, this word, curiously, was rendered *Obermann*. As a matter of tradition, the Revelation of Anakum is said to have been given by the Ava to the Karaí as if these were the names of tribes or nations; however, all serious scholars acknowledge that the the true intent of the text was to reflect the transmission of the Five Rules from the poor to the elite.

[3]In the Guaraní language, the word *tuvicha* literally means "like a father." Among the Ava, the role of *tuvicha* had no political or juridical overtones. His role, in fact, was more or less limited to serving as chief undertaker. The office was neither hierarchical nor dynastic, but rotated among the adult males of the different clans for one-year terms. Once all of the men had served, the cycle would repeat.

[4]*Ava*, like *Karaí*, is not a proper name, but the generic word in Guaraní for "man." It does not connote sex, *kuimba'e* being the word for male. It forms the root of many common words in the Guaraní lexicon: *avave*, "nobody"; *máva*, "who"; *mávapa*, "who?"; *mavandive*, "with whom", *avare*, "priest" (literally, "ex-man"), etc. The Guaraní language itself is properly called *avañe'ê* (literally, "man-speak") whereas purists still refer to the Spanish language not as *español* or *castellano*, but as *karaíñe'ê*. As noted in footnote 2, we on the Panel elected unanimously to retain *Ava* and *Karaí* as proper nouns in this translation purely out of respect for cherished tradition.

it would always be possible for the Ava[4] to carry out corrections.

I exerted much effort climbing the walls of the crater, mostly because there remained no living Ava to give me food or *chicha*. A great many cadavers bordered the cobblestone path as it reached for the sky, for this was the place where we brought our dead. Some had partially been eaten by condors, others simply lay where I had left them last winter, but now brown and frozen stiff. Because an Ava never eats alone, I could not stop.

Once I reached the plateau, I walked many nights until I arrived at the edge of the world, and I looked down from a cliff, which I now know was arid and chalky, at a formless sponge of green and red vegetation far below beneath a scorching, cold sun. I was hungry, but there was only a single llama behind me. At the foot of the great gray statue of a Karaí[5], whose arms covered the valley below from the sun, I nearly stepped on a dried llama fetus, and seeing it had no breath in it, I picked it up and began to chew on it. It too was nearly frozen. This was the first time I had ever eaten alone.

It took many more nights to reach the bottom, stumbling amid a tangle of palms and coca bushes. As the edge of the plateau behind me disappeared into the clouds, my breathing deepened. I know now, but did not know then, that I was afraid. I fell asleep beside a transparent brook in which I saw neither gold nor blood.

When I awoke, someone was standing over me, taller than an Ava, and a bit darker, with a neatly trimmed bush of hair beneath his nose and

[5]This statue is sometimes identified with the *Cristo de la Cumbre*, which sits more than 1,000 meters above the city of La Paz at the start of the road that descends to the Bolivian jungle town of Coroico. The present statue is believed to have been built in the 1960s, but the reference to a "great gray statue of a Karaí" in the Revelation certainly lends credence to the theory that another statue must have existed on the same spot for centuries beforehand.

[6]*Llahua* is the Aymara word for a man's tunic, which was fashioned out of a single piece of woven cloth and worn by passing the head through a hole in its center. The woman's cloak was, and still is, known as an *urku*. We can infer from some of Anakum's statements that the Ava's *llahuas* were all exactly the same size, and

another bit on his chin. He was not wearing a *llahua*[6], but rather a white collarless shirt that went down to his feet. Shiny black hair peeked out beneath his skullcap. He wore nothing of llama wool. I stared at his chest which was inflating and deflating like mine, and from this observation alone I knew that he could not be eaten.

My breathing resumed its normal rhythm. I remembered that when my second son was born, a member of the maize clan had left Chuguiagu during a long snowstorm, and returned the next winter to tell us that there was not far from Chuguiagu a jungle, and in that jungle, there were breathing creatures with two legs who did not wear *llahuas*, who spoke in coughs and spits, and wore only white shirts that reached their feet and skullcaps. They called themselves the Karaí.

I did not hesitate to ask a question because I knew that he could answer it truthfully and knowingly: "Are you a Karaí?"

"Yes," the creature with two legs answered. " What is your name?"

I was amazed to hear the question, and glanced around for a correcting rock and a black velvet[7] cloth, but there were none to be found. In Chuguiagu, every home had a stone and correcting cloth next to the fire, the rock as big as an adult Ava's head. I arose and as I walked towards the brook, he asked the same ques-

---

contrary to the prevailing custom among the Aymara people, the Ava's *llahua* was worn by men and women alike.

[7]Because Guaraní lacks a word for "velvet," the Spanish word *terciopelo* was used here in the original text. It literally means "third hair" or "third hide" which spiritualists claim is an allusion to Anakum's third rule: "Only ask questions that the person to whom they are posed can answer truthfully and knowingly." Some Latin Americans take the mysticism one step further because *tercero* in Buenos Aires slang (*lunfardo*) means a river formed by torrential rains in the poor back alleys of a city—an allusion, they say, to the river Choqueyapu.

[8]The Guaraní words *yapo guarã* and its negation *yapo guarã'y* occur frequently throughout the Revelation, and form what one could fairly call, without descending too deeply into dogmatism, the essential core of Anakumist doctrine. As might be expected, though, it is difficult to convey the precise sense of either of these terms in a foreign language, even one as amenable to expressing nuanced shades of meaning as English. Literally, *yapo guarã* means

tion, but in the useful[8] form: "Do you have a name?"

I answered him quickly: "I am an Ava, from Chuguiagu."

"I know," the Karaí answered, "I have heard that you exist up there." He pointed towards the cliff that I had begun to descend many nights before. "But do you have a name for yourself?"

The question had never been asked before, but it had an answer.

"No."

"Here in the jungle, everyone must have a name. Thus I shall call you Anakum." From that day forward I was known as Anakum[9].

I, too, asked the Karaí a question: "Do you have a name?" Even if a correcting rock and black velvet cloth had been nearby, there was no uselessness in this question.

"for doing" but without the accompanying sense of moral obligation that one encounters in the Bible or the Qur'an. Thus, the panel rejected "necessary" (in Guaraní, *tecotevê*) or "obligatory" (*va'erã* as a postposition) as "facially wrong," while the more neutral "convenient" was judged "inappropriate because in 1640, Padre Ruiz de Montoya in his monumental work, *Arte y bocabulario de la lengua guaraní,* translated the Spanish *conveniente cosa* (i.e., Latin *conveniens*) by *aguyyetei,* a word still in use among learned users of classical Guaraní." All published lexica of the Guaraní language support the equivalence of the postposition *guarã* to the Spanish or Portuguese adjective *útil,* thereby confirming the almost totemic significance of the word "useful" to represent the original *yapo guarã* and "useless" for *yapo guarã'y.*

[9]Various theories of the derivation of the name *Anakum* have surfaced. The most commonly accepted meaning is "I (*ana*) belonging to you (*kum*)"in classical Arabic, but if this is true it also represents something of a grammatical innovation because Arabic pronouns cannot take on possessive adjectives. The mystical and spiritual wings of our faith prefer to construe Anakum as a synaloepha of the Arabic sentence *ana aqum,* "I shall rise." Muslim propagandists, on the other hand, point out that *ana aqum* is a vulgar euphemism in Gulf Arabic meaning "my penis is becoming erect." At least one outspoken Christian critic of the Revelation has pointed out that Anakum is nothing but an alternate vocalization of the word Hebrew proper noun *Anakim,* which appears in Numbers 13:33: "And there were saw the Nephilim (the Anakim, who come from the Nephilim); and we seemed to ourselves like grasshoppers, and so we seemed to them."

"My name is Pedro Tannar[10]."

"Is this your clan?" I asked.

"No. It is my name, my own name," answered Pedro Tannar.

I remained many nights and many winters in the Jungle of the Karaí, and after mastering their language, I learned many things from Pedro Tannar. With each thing I learned from him about the Karaí, I, Anakum, learned something about myself, and the Ava, and Chuguiagu, even though Pedro Tannar was a Karaí who had not yet seen the twinkling lights of Chuguiagu nestled in its mountain crater, or the river Choqueyapu[11] whose water ran with gold and, at the times of correction, with threads of blood.

Apay[12]

I remained with Pedro Tannar in the jungle for many nights and through many rains. He had no white hair on the day he awakened me beside the brook, and he created three

---

[10] The name of Anakum's companion, which appears as either *Pedro* or *Pietru Tannar* in all of the original manuscripts, is not Arabic, but Maltese, and should properly be written as *Pietru Tan-Nar* ("Peter of the Fire"). Because of the orthographical discrepancy in the original manuscripts, the Panel voted to adopt the official spelling *Pedro Tannar* as a way of embracing both the companion's obviously Semitic background and the Hispanic world in which he shared a portion of his life with Anakum.

[11] *Choqueyapu* in Aymara means "god of gold." This river still flows from the edge of the Altiplano through the center of modern-day La Paz, where it is entombed in concrete, much to the relief of the *Paceños'* olfactory senses. The river's gold, however, has long been exhausted, every gram having been repatriated to the Old World long before Bolivia's independence, and the Choqueyapu is now no more than a trickling stream serving as the annual conduit for millions of tons of human urine and feces, not to mention countless millions of liters of toxic byproducts effusing from the leather tanneries along its banks. One Catholic apologist has tried to disprove the validity of the Revelation by arguing in a pamphlet distributed throughout the New York subway system that there is no evidence that the author of the Revelation spoke Aymara and, therefore, the repeated occurrence of the word *choqueyapu* can only be construed as a dialectal aberration of the Guaraní words *chugui yapu*, "from him [comes] a lie."

[12] "I arise" in Guaraní.

children during the time that we were together there. He was my constant companion, though it took me some time to overcome the reflex to correct Pedro Tannar, who knew nothing of the rules.[13]

Shortly after I began sleeping with him, he asked me when I was born.

No one had ever asked me when I was born. It was a useless question, for I could not have answered truthfully and knowingly. In Chuguiagu, he would have been corrected for asking it. But, we were in the jungle, and in the jungle, the ways were different.

I know that I must have been born, just as each of my five or seventeen children had been born. I know that my mother must have taken off her *llahua*, then she laid herself down on it with raised knees, as one of the women of the midwifery clan reached into her vagina to guide my head out. I did not see it, but I had seen my own children born, and it would be useless to say that I had been born in any other way.

In Chuguiagu, we had no time, so it was also useless to ask when I was born. Unlike the Karaí, we did not divide life into days, or hours, or years, certainly not into hours or seconds. No one had a birthday. We simply existed, and if we existed, we must have been born, like everyone else.

Pedro Tannar feared my lack of a birthday. He argued with me that each man had to know the date of his birth, and tried to force me to choose one, but I refused. He suggested that we honor my birth on the fourth day of the fifth month[14], as the Karaí calculated it, and to add to his comfort, I did not oppose him.

I told Pedro Tannar that "useless questions decrease comfort by leading to other useless questions. A question about a beginning always leads to a question about an end, and a question about life always leads to a question about birth or death. In Chuguiagu, we do not talk about birth or life, because then we shall eventually have

---

[13] In one manuscript, the gloss "when we met" written in Egyptian Arabic (*meta iltiqeyna*) rather than Guaraní, but there is no other authority for its inclusion in Anakum's original text.

[14] Perhaps this is an allusion to the Hebrew prophet Ezekiel, who received his divine vision "in the thirtieth year in the fourth month on the fifth of the month, as I was among the exiles by the Chebar canal." (*Ezekiel* 1:1).

to talk about death. As there is neither beginning nor end, so too there is no birth or death or life in between. Only feeling exists."

In Chuguiagu, we lived in comfort because we experienced only feeling, which did not begin and, therefore, could not end. This caused much consternation to Pedro Tannar, for whom death represented the goal of life. He did not understand that for the Ava, death was as unimportant as birth, because we only asked useful questions and corrected those who asked useless ones.

Ayurupyte[15]

Pedro Tannar's fever made his body shake and gave him headaches that made him curse in pain and vomit. He had been bitten by mosquitoes during the rainy season, and because he was weak, he was regularly sick.

"Master, why am I sick?" asked Pedro Tannar.

"Because the Karaí have many rules, but they regulate nothing except themselves."

"What am I to do, Master, to regain my health?"

"Follow the rules of the Ava," I responded.

"Teach them to me, o Master, that it may go well with me."

I spoke patiently to Pedro Tannar. "The first rule of the Ava is to promote comfort. Just as there can be no beginning without an end, my dear companion, there can be no illness without health. In Chuguiagu, there is no health or sickness. There is only comfort and discomfort."

Pedro Tannar was crying, and he lay his capless head against my chest.

"How do I find comfort, o Master?"

"Comfort is not a thing to be found, like gold or the entrails of a breathless animal. Comfort is like your breath. It simply exists." I put my arms around Pedro Tannar's body where he lay in the grass, and pushed my groin against him. I did not let him go, and he fell asleep in my arms.

When Pedro Tannar awoke, he kissed me, as he usually did, and he told me that his head was still aching. I grabbed onto him again and started breathing lightly into his left ear. He laughed like a child.

"When an Ava is in discomfort, another goes to him and holds onto him tightly, and

---

[15] "I kiss" in Guaraní.

does not let go. He will sleep in his arms, have sex with him, chew his coca[16] for him, even remain with him until death. But, he will not release his hold or leave until the discomfortable Ava says, 'I am comfortable now.' This is how we promote comfort."

Pedro Tannar looked into my eyes and kissed my lips as he said the words "I love you."

"You have much to learn, my dear companion, for the Karaí's rules are different. In Chuguiagu, each clan has a task. My father, and his father before him, and his father before him, wove cloth out of llama wool to make *llahuas*. Without our labor, everyone in Chuguiagu would be cold. My father's mother was in the maize clan, and without her there would be no *chicha* to

---

[16]Coca (*Erythroxylon coca*) is the veiny leaf of a green shrub that has been an essential part of the religious and secular lives of the Aymara and Quechua peoples for no less than three thousand years. To this day, the time for chewing coca (in Aymara, *akulliko*) is something of a sacred institution in the Andes, having the same social importance as the American coffee break. When chewed in sufficient quantities, coca reduces hunger pangs, assists in the oxygenation of one's blood at high altitudes, and induces a pleasant state of euphoria marked by both melancholy and contemplation. Each leaf contains between 0.5 and 0.9 percent of the alkaloid cocaine, as well as a host of other vitamins and alkaloids. Many of the impoverished inhabitants of Bolivia and Peru aliment themselves almost exclusively on *la hoja sagrada*, despite draconian restrictions sanctioned by the United Nations and mandated by the Drug Enforcement Administration against coca cultivation. The indigenous peoples of the Andes did not possess the chemical materials to transform coca into cocaine hydrochloride, which the Germans invented in the nineteenth century for use as a dental anesthetic and cauterizing agent. In the words of one recent Bolivian presidential candidate, "Coca bears the same resemblance to cocaine as grapes to wine."

[17]Coca chewers use *legía*, a paste or tablet composed of a base substance such as *quinoa*, potato or *camote* ash, to induce the production of saliva and to draw out the cocaine alkaloid. When the ash is mixed with cane sugar or molasses and aniseed, it is called *achura* in Aymara; when mixed with salt, it is known as *cuta*. Although European and *mestizo* Bolivians and Peruvians outwardly dismiss the chewing of coca as a repulsive *chola* habit, they generally keep supermarket-bought teabags of *mate de coca* in their cupboards to sip as an after-dinner tonic. Those from the upper echelons who

drink, and my father's father was in the *legía*[17] clan; without them we could not make *cuta* and *achura* to chew coca. My mother was born in the midwifery clan, and without her no children could be born.

From day to night, or night to day, as one chooses, there is work to be done. But, when one begins to feel discomfort, one goes to any other Ava and eats with him, or chews coca with him, or has sex with him, and if after chewing too much coca, he begins to feel a different discomfort, he goes to another Ava to drink *chicha* or have sex with him, as he likes.

Pedro Tannar asked me to bring him *chicha*. I brought him a gourd where we had just spit much chewed corn last night, and the night before, and the night before that, and we drank together as I held him in my arms. The air was warm and moist, not like in Chuguiagu, and Pedro Tannar's fever was breaking. We drank together until the sky became a sea of white stars, Pedro Tannar holding the gourd to my mouth, and me holding it to his. He vomited onto the grass, and I pulled out a wad of coca leaves and a small bit of *cuta* from my *huallquepo*.

"I cannot, o Master. I am sick, and fear I shall die."

"You do not understand the rules, my dear companion. You are in discomfort, for you do not know when to stop drinking *chicha*. Therefore, you must chew coca with me until you feel comfort again. This is the first rule."

Añandu[18]

Pedro Tannar awoke in my arms after we had chewed coca until dawn. I sought comfort by having sex with him, but Pedro Tannar refused, for he sometimes grew angry when I did not answer his questions.

"How can you not believe in God?"

"This is a useless question, my dear companion. You know that the Ava do not use the verb 'believe,' for the only belief is feeling, and what you believe in cannot be uttered because if you utter it, you control it."

Pedro Tannar was confused. "Is there a God?"

I insisted. "The question is useless."

---

chew the leaves tend to do so in private, and prefer packaged bicarbonate of soda to homemade *legía*.

[18]"I feel" in Guaraní.

Pedro Tannar grew angry, and I held him tightly for much time, but soon he kissed my lips with the words "I love you."

"Please tell me, o Master, what is God?"

"What you say is unutterable. This is part of the second rule."

"Teach me, o Master, my life is in your hands."

"You still do not understand the rules, my dear companion. An Ava can only speak truthfully and knowingly. If you ask someone how his health is, and he responds 'I am fine' by reflex, although he is feeling discomfort, he is not speaking truthfully, and is subject to correction. Do you understand?"

Pedro Tannar nodded, though he still did not grasp the meaning of my words.

"In the same manner, an Ava does not speak about the unutterable, which is more than the universe, for he cannot speak knowingly about something of which he is but a tiny fraction of an atom.[19] Our feeling does not control the unutterable; rather, the unutterable controls our feeling."

I grabbed Pedro Tannar again by the shoulders for he was crying, and I rocked him to sleep like an infant. When he awoke, still in my arms, he took no *chicha* or coca, but insisted on mastering the second rule.

---

[19] The word that we have translated as "tiny fraction of an atom"— *thurai* (with the final letter bearing the accent) – is *hapax legomenon* in the Revelation as well as the extant literature in Guaraní and Spanish. The early translations of the Revelation in the European languages treated it as a proper noun and did not even attempt to translate it. However, advances in comparative Semitic linguistics have proven beyond the shadow of a doubt that the interdental and silbative consonants (*s, sh, th, dh, z*) are interchangeable. Thus, the most plausible explanation is that this unique word derives from the colloquial form of the classical Arabic *dharra*, which occurs in two consecutive Qur'anic verses to convey the sense of a particle of matter insusceptible of human measurement: "And whosoever does an atom's weight of good shall see it, and whosoever does an atom's weight of evil shall see it" (*Qur'an* XCIX:7-8). The word was indigenized by the addition of the Guaraní diminutive suffix -*i*, thereby assuring its absorption as an Anakumist concept. It bears noting that some commentators see in the word *thurai* a reference to "maize" (in classical Arabic, *dhurra*), while yet others draw an etymological link to *thaura*, Arabic for "revolution."

"I do not understand, o Master," Pedro Tannar cried out. "Please help me."

I, Anakum, sat and looked at him. "In the jungle, you have tall towers adorned with luxurious stones and metals from which sounds are sent out to beckon the Karaí to feel or, as you say, 'think of' or 'remember' or 'pray to' the unutterable. You have special buildings in which these feelings are spoken, and outside of which the feelings evaporate with the morning mist. You have time and calendars, and many rules concerning the days and hours when the prayers must be recited, and discomforting athletic exercises that the Karaí are compelled to repeat at these appointed times. If there are certain days and hours when you pray, this means that there are other days and hours, even entire nights, when you do not do so. This is not our way, for it violates the first and second rules."

"What, then, is the second rule, o Master?" asked Pedro Tannar.

"Speak truthfully and knowingly, my dear companion. Feel the unutterable as the unutterable exists, in every fiber of your body, for at every blink of your eyelid, it is there. Every heartbeat, every drop of blood coursing through your body, every breath, is the most that an Ava can know of the unutterable. But the unutterable is more than everything! You feel the unutterable as it treads lightly over the human body like a spider.[20] Do not think, or believe, or recite, my dear companion, just feel."

But Pedro Tannar was confused, for to the Karaí, the un-

---

[20] This sentence, immensely significant to the formulation of Anakum's theosophy, appears entirely in Guaraní without any bastardizing Castilian influences or Semitic loan words. To fully understand the meaning, it bears examining the original text, for Anakum was here showing a jocular side by engaging in a brilliant play on words: "*Ne ñandu ichupe oguatapy'i ava rete ári ñandúicha.*" (emphasis added). The word *ñandu* can mean the verb "feel" or the abstract noun "feeling," but also "spider" or "ostrich." The latter animal does not fit the delicacy of Anakum's allusion, and thus we, like all the earlier translations, adopt "spider" as the intended reference. Muslim apologists often use this verse in their attacks on Anakum's Revelation, citing "the parable of those who protect themselves without Allah is like that of the spider that protects itself with a house, but the spider's house is truly the flimsiest of houses—if they only knew" (*Qur'an* XXIX:41).

utterable had a special name, and a special building, and could only be felt at special times and with special movements. I had to drink much *chicha* and chew much coca to regain comfort.

Over the many years in the jungle, Pedro Tannar always called the unutterable *Allah* or *Dios*, and though we slept in each other's arms every night, he sometimes refused to have sex with me unless I consented to use a name for the unutterable. I objected again and again because it was against our rules to speak unknowingly or untruthfully, and even though correction was not practiced among the Karaí, I could not find comfort if I broke any of the Ava's rules.

It was not until Pedro Tannar and I returned together to Chuguiagu with his daughter and his sister that he called the unutterable by another (or "the other")[21] name.

After many nights sleeping in each other's arms, Pedro Tannar asked me how to say "Father" in the Ava's language, which he had not yet mastered.

"*Tuva*."

"Then we shall call the unutterable *Tuva*, for he revealed himself to you as a father makes himself known to his son."

"My dear companion, still you have not learned the second rule. Using this name would be untruthful, for my father sometimes feels discomfort, but the unutterable is beyond comfort and discomfort."

Pedro Tannar cried, and hugged me, and did not release his hold. His chest vibrated as tears fell down his cheeks. Then, as a parrot nestled in the tree shading us, he looked in my eyes and asked, "O Mas-

---

[21] Classical Guaraní has neither a definite nor an indefinite article.

[22] Each of the five extant manuscripts of the Revelation record Pedro Tannar's question in bilingual form: the words "O Master, how do you say" are in Guaraní ("*Tuvicha, mba'éichapa ere*"), and the appellation "Father of all" is in Arabic (*waalad al-jamii*). Thus, the authenticity of this text is beyond challenge.

[23] Nearly all the members of the panel, including this reporter, agreed that Anakum's response to Pedro Tannar's question was added by a later redactor at pains to explain the derivation of the divine name. It is present in all five manuscripts and in all translations and, for that reason, has been retained as part of the original text. Chief among the indices of its inauthenticity is the author's obvious lack of familiarity with the rules of Guaraní morphology. The proper

ter, how do you say 'Father of all'?"[22]

"*Tupã*."[23]

"So it shall be," he said as he kissed my lips with the words "I love you." "We shall use the name *Tupã* between us."

Feeling Pedro Tannar's discomfort, I agreed to use the name *Tupã* between us whenever he wanted to talk about the unutterable.

---

rendering of "father of all" in Guaraní is *oparu*, which comes close to the urban Brazilian pronunciation of the Portuguese *eu paro* ("I stand" or "I stop"). Proceeding from the premise that the "homonymous replication of the unutterable's revealed name in a somewhat clichéd Portuguese declaration cannot with any degree of scholarly or theological integrity be dismissed as a mere coincidence," one Brazilian philosopher of Greek extraction, Dr. Aliquis Notabém, has ventured a complex yet intriguing theory to explain the spread of a curious Anakumist cultural phenomenon in his revolutionary text, *Noções da verdade revelada*. For the last twenty years or so—during which Anakumism has gained some eight million converts in Brazil alone—followers of the Revelation have been observed assembling to offer comfort to one another at nearly every signed busstop (*parada de ônibus*) in Rio de Janeiro, São Paulo, and the other major metropoles. Professor Notabém posits that the Revelation has taken such deep root among non-Guaraní and non-Arabic speakers because its message unexpectedly reverberates in even the most mundane circumstances of its adherents' secular lives. His reasoning goes thus: Because Pedro Tannar's question ("O Master, how do you say 'Father of all'?") is uniformly accepted as an authentic text, and because the messenger to whom the unutterable chose to entrust the Revelation was a native speaker of Guaraní, it logically follows that the true revealed name of the unutterable must be the correct Guaraní rendering of *Waalad al-Jamii*. Thus, when a Brazilian declares *eu paro*, which sounds almost exactly the same as the Guaraní *oparu*, he is on a deeper, spiritual level giving emphatic testimony to the unutterable: "Bearing in mind that *de ônibus* is a direct borrowing from the Latin *de omnibus*, 'for everyone,' and *parada* is the *substantivum loci* of the verb *eu paro*, we can only conclude that the custom of Anakumists throughout Brazil greeting one another with the words *eu paro na parada de ônibus* (literally, "I stand at the busstop") has acquired the principally spiritual and liturgical meaning of 'Tupã, in Tupã's place, for everyone.'" Yet another theory is that the redactor was alluding to the word *Tupã*, the Guaraní's god of thunder, whose name the Jesuit missionaries used in the catechism when referring to God the Father.

Añe'êyevy[24]

When the rains stopped, Pedro Tannar recovered from his tremors and headaches. He felt comfort as I put my seed into the palm of his hand, for we had decided to share my sperm, and he kissed me with the words "I love you." He did not want me to see his wife uncovered, and could not have sex with her if he looked into her face. Therefore, his discomfort quickly returned, and he showed me his back and crossed his arms in front of his chest.

I held Pedro Tannar in my arms until night, when the mosquitoes were swarming around our naked bodies. He rolled over and looked into my eyes.

"O Master, do you love me?"

"This is a useless question." He made his deep eyes contract into almonds, and started to roll over, but I grabbed him and held him tightly to my chest. I, Anakum, said: "If there is a beginning, there must also be an end. Likewise, if I love, I must also hate."

Tears rolled down Pedro Tannar's cheeks as he shook his head and dropped his face towards the grass. "I do not understand, o Master. Please tell me the other rules quickly that I may learn them by heart and recite them as you do."

"We have not completed the second rule, my dear companion. Do you remember it?"

"Yes. Speak truthfully and knowingly."

"You have spoken well. What is the first rule?"

"Promote comfort."

"Correct again. When you join these two rules, you arrive at the third: Only ask questions that the person to whom they are posed can answer truthfully and knowingly."

Then I told Pedro Tannar that when I left my home in Chuguiagu, my father asked me whither I was going.

"I could not answer, 'To find a woman so that I may create children and that correction might continue among the Ava,' for I did not know whether women existed beyond Chuguiagu. Therefore, I answered with the only words I knew to be truthful: 'I am traveling to the place where the sun sleeps.'"

Pedro Tannar was still in discomfort, and we drank *chicha*, then chewed coca, well into the next day.

"O Master, why do you not love me?"

---

[24] "I speak again" or "I repeat" in Guaraní.

"This too is a useless question, my dear companion. In Chuguiagu, such a question would earn you a swift correction."

"Then you do love me?"

"Your questions are useless."

Pedro Tannar began to cry again, and he buried his head in my chest. I hugged his buttocks tightly, and his penis became like a stone. I hugged him more tightly, but he still could not ejaculate.

We walked arm in arm into town, and Pedro Tannar took me to his family's house, where we spit maize[25] into the *chicha* gourd and chewed more coca. He had sex with his wife on a large bed, covering himself with his *llahua* so that the mosquitoes would not drink his blood, and he created another daughter. On the same day, I, Anakum, had sex with Pedro Tannar's first daughter whom he called Amal, and we created a son whom we called Entumkulu, also known as

---

[25] The word for "maize" in the original text is the Guaraní word *avati*. Because Pedro here did not use the Arabic word *dhurra*, those commentators who argue that the term *thurai* in the Book of Añandu means "a little kernel of corn" instead of "a tiny fraction of an atom" are clearly mistaken.

[26] It is impossible to ascertain from the text itself whether Entumkulu was born during the sojourn in the Jungle of the Karaí, or after Anakum's return with Pedro Tannar to Chuguiagu. Debate continues to rage in the scholarly community over the name's meaning. Relying on the absence of doubled strong consonants in Guaraní, the vast majority of the panel's theologians and philologists agree that the intended meaning of Entumkulu derives from a dialectal variation of the classical Arabic *antum kullun*, but they split about evenly on the question of whether the pronoun *kullun* refers to inanimate objects (i.e., "you are everything") or to living beings ("you are everyone"). During deliberations, other experts insisted that *entum* must be interpreted purely as the second person plural pronoun in classical Arabic, and flatly reject any analogies to its use as a formal second person singular along the lines of the German *Sie* or the French *vous*, thus preferring the meaning "you (plural) are everything" or "you (plural) are everyone." These latter academics rely heavily on the explanatory gloss "also known as Peêpa" to buttress their argument in favor of a plural subject, for in Guaraní, the word *peêpa* has only a single possible meaning, the pronominal "you (plural) all." Their argument is weakened by the absence of this gloss, or indeed of any reference at all to the name Peêpa, in the manuscript known as *La*

Peêpa.[26] Amal understood the rules, thus she broke her hymen with her own finger, carefully washing away all trace of blood before inserting my seed into her vagina.[27]

Pedro Tannar spent much time in my arms. "O Master, how many rules are there?"

I, Anakum, raised my right hand. "Five."[28]

"Please teach me, o Master, for I am in your hands."

"Make certain that you never cause blood to spill forth from another being that visibly breathes by inflating and deflating its lungs."

"Is there more, o Master?"

Florida, which is the second most complete and, *ergo,* one of the most reliable witnesses of the original text of the Revelation. One heretical sect, founded in Lebanon, but with a few thousand adherents among the gauchos and blue-collar workers of Argentina, Uruguay, and southern Brazil, interprets the naming of Anakum's first son conceived in exile as an implicit overruling of Anakum's fourth rule, for the Arabic can also mean "you, eat!" *(entum* being the emphatic pronoun "you (plural)," and *kulu* the second person plural imperative of the verb *akala,* "eat"). Whatever the linguistic derivation of Entumkulu, it is abundantly clear his name confirms the intentional shaping of the Revelation to appeal particularly to the Arabic-speaking world.

[27] The word translated as "vagina" is *taco,* which is Guaraní for "tree stump," although it is also used in vulgar speech to refer to the female pudenda.

[28] The Guaraní word found in the standard accepted text is *po,* which means "hand." It is today used in the vernacular with the meaning "five," presumably because a hand has five fingers. In the classical language, only words for the first four numbers exist: *peteî,* "one"; *mokõi,* "two"; *mbohapy,* "three"; and *irundy,* "four." We are aware of no classical Guaraní texts in which the word *po* alone appears in the numerical sense. This is a significant doctrinal point because several translations have rendered *po* as "one" (e.g., the Kuwait Arabic translation [*wahid*] and the Teheran edition in Farsi [*yek*]). On the basis of this mistranslation, members of the Monocanonite sect, which originated in Saudi Arabia and has spread throughout the Persian Gulf and the Fertile Crescent, maintain that Anakum's hand motion and concomitant use of the monosyllabic response "*Po*" prove that Tupã revealed only a single rule, of which the remaining four are mere subsets. For sake of completeness, we also note that the Qum edition translates *po* as *do,* meaning "two" in Farsi, but the panel dismisses this as a typesetting error.

"At the beginning of each rainy season, bring the goldsmith all of the gold that you have not given to other Ava, so that he may melt it down and spill it into the river whence it came."

"Is there yet another rule?"

I, Anakum, raised my open hand, and told him again, "Only five."

Pedro Tannar caught a fish in the brook, and brought it to me as it flipped in his hands.

"Can we eat it, o Master? Here we have neither *ch'uño* nor *tunta*." [29]

I, Anakum, answered in comfort: "You know the rule, my dear companion."

"Yes, o Master, we may not cause blood to spill forth from another animal that visibly breathes by inflating and deflating its lungs. But, this fish does not have lungs that I can feel."

"Leave it in the sun, and eat it."

After Pedro Tannar and I had returned to Chuguiagu, and after we had created more sons and daughters, a young girl of the *legía* clan called Marangatu[30] was trying to cut a piece of flesh from a dead Ava's arm, for we had chosen on that day to drink *chicha*, chew coca and have sex in her house. Seeing that the blade was dull, a young boy named Vaca Ra'y brought in a sharp knife, but as he rushed holding it by the handle, he jabbed Marangatu in the thumb causing a few drops of blood to appear.

Pedro Tannar was still learning the rules. Therefore, on that day, he took hold of

---

[29] On the Altiplano, where food is scarce, there are more than two hundred varieties of potatoes and starchy tubers. To preserve potatoes in the region's extreme cold, the indigenous peoples have devised two methods of dehydrating potatoes: one by wrapping them in straw and burying them in the earth for a few days, resulting in *ch'uño*, the other by placing them under ice-cold running water for up to one month, yielding the lily-white and considerably more expensive *tunta*.

[30] Guaraní for "blessed."

[31] This is a fine example of the difficulties encountered in textual criticism. In three of the extant manuscripts and about sixty percent of the printed versions, the beginning of this first sentence reads "*Ha upéicha, amo árape, o mbotyryry mitã'i osapukáivo **nasiatahuve**...*" The word *nasiatahu* is not Guaraní, but classical Arabic for "his forelock," and occurs in one of the earliest revelations in the Qur'an: "Does he not know that Allah sees? Let him beware! If he does

the young boy, shouting, by the forelock[31], put his arms around his shoulders and led him to the hearth. I, Anakum, asked the boy if he was in comfort, and he responded "Yes."

When Yvaga Ra'y[32] was kneeling with his nose touching the ground, Pedro Tannar covered the boy's head with the black velvet cloth and recited three times the rule with which the boy had

---

not desist, we will drag him by the *forelock*—a lying, sinful forelock. Then let him call to his comrades: We will call on the angels of punishment! No, heed him not, but prostrate, and bring yourself closer!" (*Qur'an* XCVI:14-19). In the remaining two manuscripts, *ñatiûto'uve* ("let the mosquitoes eat more!") appears in place of *nasiatahuve*, and this reading has been adopted by a quarter of the translated versions of the Revelation. The panel concluded that the Arabic-speaking Pedro Tannar, clearly familiar with Islamic terminology, was probably making a Qur'anic allusion and therefore, decided that the intended reference was "forelock." Furthermore, they dismissed *ñatiûto'uve* as an honest attempt by the amanuenses of El-Wadih and El-Uthmaniyya to correct what they had perceived as an error in pronunciation or spelling. The panel buttressed its final conclusion on this word with the observation that among most Anakumists, the custom to this day is for men to let their bangs reach their eyebrows to give witness to the world that they, like this young boy in Chuguiagu, stand ready at any time to be corrected *pro maiorem bonum publicum*. However, particularly in Saudi Arabia and the Arabian Gulf, where Anakumists are known to have made significant clandestine inroads among the disenfranchised urban youth, the latest craze in tonsorial fashion is to crop the forelock as closely as possible to the scalp, leaving just a slight upward, though visible, tuft far too short for anyone to grasp.

[32] All extant manuscripts except *Hollywood Eight* reflect what must have been Anakum's intentional play on the boy's name: *Vaca Ra'y* is Guaraní for "son of a cow" while its near homophone, *Yvaga Ra'y*, means "son of heaven."

[33] The text does not specify which rule Yvaga Ra'y failed to respect and for which he had to be corrected. Most commentators take the common-sense view that the boy suffered correction because he jabbed Marangatu's thumb, thereby violating the fourth rule: "Make certain that you never cause blood to spill forth from another being that visibly breathes by inflating and deflating its lungs." However, those who ascribe mystical powers to Anakum and his companion call on the grammatical "rule of the last occurring referent" to interpret this passage as proof that

not complied.[33]   After each recitation, Pedro Tannar hit the back of the boy's head with the correcting stone, not lightly but with just enough force to prevent blood from spilling forth.

When Pedro Tannar had recited the rule three times, I, Anakum, heard the boy's skull crack, and he tumbled to the side. The *tuvicha* carried him to the banks of the river Choqueyapu, where he slit the boy's neck in a single quick motion, letting all of his blood drip into the water whence our gold came. Then he lay the boy's body on the road near the edge of the crater, among the other cadavers, but vultures and some of the Ava quickly ate up his body, for the boy was very young, and his flesh very sweet.

Ambokaraíguasu[34]

Pedro Tannar awoke in the grass beside me, for we had just had sex.

Pedro Tannar *foresaw* that the young boy would violate the rule "speak truthfully and knowingly" when Anakum asked him if he was in comfort, and led him to the hearth *before* the boy answered "Yes," which was the useless act for which he was ultimately corrected. In his book *Truth About-Face*, a noted American theologian who adopted the pseudonym Carl de Dapper argues: "Which boy would not fear the eventuality of correction for the harmless, accidental thumb-jabbing of Marangatu? Tupã's messenger saw what each of us instinctively feels when reading this passage: that Pedro Tannar acted precipitously by concluding that the boy had to be corrected. By any other interpretation, the verse "And I asked the boy if he was in comfort, and he responded 'Yes'" is rendered nugatory." This interpretation has been cited by certain lawyers in the United States for the proposition that correction ought not to be administered in the case of accidental or negligent blood-lettings, but the Anakumist mainstream has thoroughly dismissed this view as contrary to the plain text of the Revelation.

[34] "I correct" in Guaraní. Literally it means "I make (you) a great man" or a "leader"; hence, classical Guaraní lexica offer this verb as an equivalent of the Spanish *corregir,* which has the sense of "correct" on the one hand, and "rule" or "lead" (thus also to "chastise" or "moderate") on the other. In the original text of the Revelation, Anakum alternates between the substantival forms of three verbs when referring to the key theological concept of correction. They are, in order of frequency: *mboheco* (literally, to make "delicate" or "refined"), *mbokaraíguasu,* and *myatyrõ* (to "arrange" or "repair").

"Is there forgiveness, o Master?"

I, Anakum, responded: "No. Remember, my dear companion, there can be no beginning without an end, nor can there be forgiveness unless there be sin. I say to you, there is no sin, and there is no forgiveness. All such things are useless."

Pedro Tannar continued to fiddle with a strand of amber beads. He glanced up at the sky, and began to cry again, so I hugged his body to mine and rocked him back and forth. He kissed my lips with the words "I love you" many times.

"Please make me understand, o Master."

"You do not speak truthfully and knowingly, my dear companion. For the Karaí, forgiveness is the mother of sin. It is an Ava's enemy, not his friend."

But Pedro Tannar continued to weep and to play with his beads.

"You the Karaí go out into the world and touch money, and you speak untruthfully and unknowingly. With tears and murmurings, you confess the rules you break, but by reciting words that you do not feel and kneeling and rising a few times, you forgive yourselves. When night comes, you return to do useless things, arrogantly waiting for dawn to arrive so that you can confess and be forgiven once again. Thus your useless acts multiply, and the Ava is reduced to nothing, for he is never corrected."

Pedro Tannar's eyes opened wide. "And thus we proclaim a final judgment?"

"You yourself are now seeking correction, my dear companion."

With these words, Pedro Tannar burst into tears and left me, Anakum, alone beside the brook. Seeing that he was in discomfort, I put on my *llahua* and ran after him, hugging him beneath a tall tower whence a storm of discomforting sounds pierced the air. I followed him through the gate, but he told me I could not enter because my penis was uncircumcised. I waited until Pedro Tannar emerged, playing again with his beads and smiling, and I grabbed him by the shoulders, hugging him as we walked back to the brook, where we removed our *llahuas* and had sex.

Ayuyevy[35]

---

[35]"I come back" or "I return" in Guaraní.

After enduring many rains in the jungle, I returned to Chuguiagu. Pedro Tannar, his daughter Amal, his son Zulam Ben Pedro, my son Entumkulu also called Peêpa and their companions and children came along. It was a slow trek, and by the time we reached the summit, Pedro Tannar had taken ill. He found it difficult to breathe, but I hugged him to my body in the shadow of the giant man whose arms guarded the descent into the valley, and we chewed much coca but drank little *chicha*. Certain that Pedro Tannar would feel discomfort if we remained there through the frigid cold of the night, I, Anakum, grabbed him by one shoulder, and my son Entumkulu grabbed him by the other, and we carried him across the windy plateau as the sun departed to resume its sleep.

When we arrived at the edge of the crater, and saw the twinkling lights of Chuguiagu below, I asked Pedro Tannar if he was feeling comfort again.

"Yes, o Master, to be with you among the Ava is the greatest comfort for me."

I responded, "My dear companion, with only a few words, you have violated the first two rules."

He cried and said he was tired. Thus, I insisted that we rest, and finish drinking a large gourd of *chicha*, and chew coca, and dance, and sing, and have sex. When we awoke in one another's arms, we descended along the road where I had seen many cadavers when I left Chuguiagu, but where nothing but low hills of dust now remained.

The sun resumed its sleep when we entered the house I had left behind so many years before. My father was awake, and we called my son, who was living in an adjacent house. The goldsmith came to visit also, bringing with him a gourd of *chicha*. Together we finished it quickly to increase our comfort, but we had brought much more *chicha* with us, and coca too, and we drank until the sun arose, singing, and dancing, and chewing coca, and having sex.

The next morning, the goldsmith went to the river Choqueyapu and searched for gold. He brought the nuggets back to his workshop, and melted them down into bars, each one the size of his hand. Because he knew that the highest number was five, he brought five shining bars of gold to my house after the sun went to sleep. He gave one

117

each to me and Amal because of Entumkulu, and three to Pedro Tannar.

Pedro Tannar objected, asking the goldsmith, "Why do you give me three, when my Master only receives one?"

The goldsmith answered quickly but comfortably, "This is the fifth rule." And Pedro Tannar began to cry, because he had forgotten the fifth rule. Thus, the goldsmith and I, as well as Amal, ran to Pedro Tannar, hugging him to ourselves, but as soon as the time for sleep arrived, Pedro Tannar took the goldsmith to his bed, and he remained in the goldsmith's embrace, chewing coca and drinking *chicha* and having sex, until Pedro Tannar regained comfort.

Each day thereafter, after the goldsmith had found gold in the river Choqueyapu and melted it down, he brought one bar of gold to each mother and father for each child they had created, but regardless of how many children each mother and father had, the goldsmith could produce no more than five bars of gold in a single day, for the goldsmith did not know the way the Karaí counted, but only the way the Ava counted. As for me, I had eighteen children by the Karaí's calculation, but in Chuguiagu this equaled five; thus, by the end of the rainy season, I received five bars of gold, Amal received one bar of gold, and Pedro Tannar received three bars of gold.

On the first day of the rainy season, I became *tuvicha* again. There were not yet any corpses among us; thus, I had no job to fulfill.

That day, the goldsmith went around to each Ava, male and female, and collected the gold bars that each had received—one for each child—at the beginning of the previous rainy season. He said to each of them only one word—"Speak!"—and when the Ava heard this word, they each gave an account of all the gold that they had not given to, or received from, another Ava since the previous rainy season. Once the number was confirmed—and it was never more than five—the goldsmith wrapped the bars in his *llahua* and took them back to his workshop to melt them down that very same day. With great care, the goldsmith then poured the molten gold into a bucket of cold water, which immediately froze into small nuggets, which he alone carried downhill to the river Choqueyapu in order to fulfill the rule of returning the gold to the water whence it had come.

But Pedro Tannar was a Karaí, who from his childhood knew buying and selling. He found it impossible to understand how the Ava ate, drank, chewed coca, danced, and had sex in anyone's house, all at any time they wished and without payment of any kind. Once, when he wanted to return to the jungle to purchase a supply of coca with one of his bars of gold, I, Anakum, stopped him.

"My dear companion, do you not yet know the fifth rule?"

"Yes, o Master: 'At the beginning of each rainy season, bring the goldsmith all of the gold that you have not given to other Ava, so that he may melt it down and spill it into the river whence it came.' But, why is this useful?" Pietru said this because he was sad.

"Because it is the rule."

"But why, o Master, is it the rule?"

"Because it is useful, my dear companion. If you practice this rule, you will have mastered all the others."

We lived in Chuguiagu for a long time, but the cold, thin air made Pedro Tannar frequently uncomfortable so that he longed to return to his home in the humid jungle. On the night before his departure, I took him in my arms and hugged him tightly, for he was again crying.

"You have learned everything I can reveal, my dear companion. Return whence you came. When you are again among the Karaí, for that is Tupã's will, eat, and drink, and chew coca, and dance, and sing, but in everything you do, whether outside or inside, practice the rules and soon all the Karaí will join you."

All of Pedro Tannar's children except Dalam remained in Chuguiagu, and they had sex with the Ava and created more children, and every day they practiced the rules.

Part Three

JUSTICE IS BLIND

JUSTICE IS BLIND

IN THE SUPREME COURT OF THE UNITED STATES

On Writ of Certiorari to the United States
Court of Appeals for the Fifth Circuit

EDWIN FRANCIS VANCE, Petitioner
v. WARDEN, LOUISIANA STATE PENITENTIARY,
Respondent
Case No. _____

On behalf of the Petitioner, Professor Dylan Hardwick and
Andrew Sear, 202 Burgundy Street, New Orleans, Louisiana,
and on behalf of the Respondent, the Honorable District Attorney of Orleans Parish, State of Louisiana, 701 South White
Street, New Orleans, Louisiana.

JUSTICE A.B. delivered the opinion of the Court. JUS-
TICE C.D., joined by JUSTICE E.F., filed an opinion concurring in the judgment only. JUSTICE G.H. filed an opinion
dissenting.

MATERIAL FACTS

Somewhat surprisingly for a case of this magnitude, the material facts are not in dispute.

Edwin Francis Vance was born on August 15, 1964 in a middle-class neighborhood in Metairie, Louisiana. He attended parochial schools—first St. Edward the Confessor in Metairie, followed by Christian Brothers Academy in City Park—until the age of seventeen, when he accepted a full scholarship to pursue a baccalaureate program in business administration at Tulane University. During his college years, he distinguished himself academically, graduating with a cumulative grade-point average of 3.72, and began what he himself has termed a "fanatical devotion" to swimming.

Mr. Vance toyed with the idea of going to seminary for the ultimate purpose of seeking ordination into the Roman Catholic priesthood. Indeed, he spent the summer of his sophomore year at Tulane building a schoolhouse in rural El Salvador with an evangelical Catholic group but, upon his return to Louisiana, renewed a relationship with "his childhood sweetheart," Stella Carruthers, also of Metairie. He proposed to her on Christmas Eve 1985.

Disillusioned by the "accusatory tone" of the pre-Cana classes his fiancée was compelled to attend as a condition of their marriage, Mr. Vance gradually distanced himself from the Roman Catholic Church. Though the couple was indeed married in a Mass at St. Louis Cathedral in July 1986, when each of Mr. Vance's three children—Sammy, Jonathan and Rachel—was born, he expressed a "grave reluctance" to have them baptized but, ultimately, and in each case, gave in to his wife's pleas to "put the kids right before God."

Immediately after his graduation from Tulane, Mr. Vance joined the staff of his father's haberdashery. Shortly before his marriage to Stella, he accepted an entry-level position with a national conglomerate as a life insurance salesman.

His "drive to succeed" caused him to advance rapidly, "earning the envy of his coworkers and the discomfort of his supervisors," and three months before his marriage, he opened up a one-man insurance agency in a strip mall on Gentilly Boulevard in New Orleans.

Early on the evening of November 1, 1994, Mr. Vance came home to his shotgun cottage on Annunciation Street between Austerlitz and Constantinople Streets in Uptown New Orleans. Accompanying him was Josephine Colette, whom he described at the trial as the "intended bearer of my next three children." He placed on the coffee table a bag containing three pints of ice cream—chocolate chip for Sammy, pralines and cream for Jonathan, and pistachio "with the nuts" for Stella and the infant Rachel—around which "the kids swarmed as they kissed" their father. Hearing the commotion, Stella came out of the kitchen, still clad in an apron, and exclaimed, "Oh, I didn't know we were having guests tonight." She ordered the two oldest children to take their baby sister into the bedroom. Mr. Vance then strolled over to the television cabinet "to pull out a really special bottle of vintage Bordeaux...and the nice crystal glasses reserved for company."

As always, Mr. Vance unscrewed the cork, and when he had finished tasting the wine and filling the three glasses, he announced to his wife, "I'm so glad you're finally meeting Josephine. I intend to have more children with her." Mr. Vance and Josephine raised their glasses in a toast, but Stella dropped hers to the ground and shrieked: "How can you hate me so much?"

At this point, Mr. Vance excused himself and went into the kitchen, whence he called out: "Stella, please come in here." She rose from the sofa, and Josephine followed. In the kitchen, Mr. Vance instructed Stella to kneel at the foot of the stove. She complied without uttering any protest or asking any further questions. Josephine testified that "Stella wasn't crying or nothing...she was just staring at the ground like she was waiting for something she was just gonna have to grin and bear." After "carefully" covering his wife's head with a black velvet cloth, Mr. Vance struck her three times on the back of the skull with a *molcajete* (a traditional mortar made out of heavy volcanic rock which is used to make guacamole and Mexican sauces) which he and Stella had purchased on their tenth-anniversary trip to Mexico City. Between each blow, in what Josephine described at trial as a "calm, calibrated voice," Mr. Vance recited the following verses: "Speak truthfully and knowingly. Only ask questions that the person to whom they are posed can answer truthfully and knowingly."

After the third blow, Stella tumbled to the side, and Mr. Vance returned with Josephine to the living room. They continued drinking their wine and munching on macadamia nuts; in Josephine's words, "the kids was just enjoying their ice cream in the bedroom." When Mr. Vance had picked up the shattered glass and finished drinking his Bordeaux, he called the New Orleans Police and said, "I have corrected my wife Stella. She is no longer breathing. If it's not too much bother, please come to take her away."

When the medical team and the police arrived, Mr. Vance was washing out the wine glasses. The forensic team found the traces of finely ground coca leaves and a box of baking soda on the coffee table, as well as an unopened carton containing one hundred teabags of *mate de coca* which Mr. Vance and Stella had bought at the duty-free shop on their return from a vacation in La Paz, Bolivia.

Stella was pronounced dead on arrival at Southern Baptist Hospital. The autopsy, conduced by the Medical Examiner, revealed that Stella had died of cerebral swelling caused by internal bleeding as a result of a massive and sustained head trauma.

PROCEDURAL HISTORY

After taking Mr. Vance into custody and advising him of his *Miranda* rights, the police arrested Mr. Vance and charged him under section 14:30(A)(7) of the Louisiana Revised Statutes, which defines first-degree murder as the killing of a human being when the offender "has the specific intent to kill and is engaged in the activities prohibited by R.S. 14:107(C)(1)." The prohibited activities to which the statute refers are the "ritualistic mutilation, dismemberment or torture of a human as part of a ceremony, rite, initiation, observance, performance or practice[.]" He was also charged with two counts of possession of a controlled substance (i.e., the coca leaf residue and the *mate de coca* teabags) in violation of section 40:967(F)(1)(a) of the Louisiana Revised Statutes, but the District Attorney, exercising his statutory discretion, chose not to pursue these charges.

A grand jury was promptly convened by the Criminal District Court of Orleans Parish, and the jurors indicted Mr. Vance on one count of first-degree murder. The indictment was properly endorsed a "true bill" and signed by the foreman of the grand jury.

According to Mr. Vance's own testimony at pre-trial motions, the public defender spent "four or five hours" with Mr. Vance in Orleans Parish prison the day before the scheduled arraignment and tried to convince him to plead not guilty by reason of insanity. He also informed Mr. Vance that he had already initiated preliminary negotiations with the District Attorney to drop the state's intent to seek the death penalty in exchange for Mr. Vance's guilty plea, and although the District Attorney did not appear to be interested in bargaining, the public defender felt confident that he could—again, in Mr. Vance's recollection of the conversation—"push his frat brother against the wall and do some down-home arm twisting to get him to agree." Mr. Vance rejected his attorney's advice and, at his arraignment before the Honorable Judge Patrick McCarthy, entered a plea of not guilty.

The guilt phase of the trial began on Thursday, March 14, 1996 and lasted eight days. Among the state's witnesses was Josephine Colette, whom the District Attorney agreed not to charge with conspiracy and possession of a controlled substance (i.e., Xanax), and who was subject to vigorous cross-examination by the public defender. In the course of eliciting testimony from the police officers who responded to Mr. Vance's call on the night of the incident, the District Attorney tried to introduce a videotape of the crime scene after Mr. Vance's arrest. The public defender contemporaneously objected to its admissibility. In addition, during his questioning of the Medical Examiner, the District Attorney sought to introduce fifty-seven color photographs taken during Stella Vance's autopsy, but again, the public defender objected. On both occasions, the trial court sustained the public defender's objections on the ground that "the probative value of such graphic evidence is far outweighed by the danger of irreparable prejudice to the defendant."

The defense's final witness was Mr. Vance himself. Before allowing the examination to begin, Judge McCarthy conducted an extensive voir dire outside the presence of the jury to ensure that Mr. Vance's waiver of the privilege against self-incrimination was voluntary and knowing:

BY THE COURT, THE HONORABLE JUDGE MC-CARTHY PRESIDING: Mr. Vance, it is my understanding that you wish to testify on your behalf. Is that correct?

BY THE DEFENDANT: Yes, Sir, it is.

BY THE COURT: Do you understand that in this trial or any other trial you are never required to say anything in your own defense?

A: Yes, Sir.

Q: ...and that you enjoy a privilege against self-incrimination under the Fifth Amendment of the Constitution that no one—not this Court, not the prosecutor, no one—can take away from you?

A: Yes, Sir.

Q: And you know that you and your lawyer can sit there all day and smile or stick your tongues out at the jurors and say absolutely nothing, and put on absolutely no shred of evidence, and the state still has to bear the burden of proving all the elements of their case beyond a reasonable doubt?

A: Yes, Sir, I know that.

Q: Mr. Vance, can you explain the privilege against self-incrimination in your own words?

A: Well—umm—it means that the state can't compel you to give testimony against yourself, that it has to try to prove the charge against you through other means, I mean, other evidence.

Q: So, do you wish to waive your constitutional privilege against self-incrimination – that is, your Fifth Amendment right?

A: Yes, Your Honor, I do wish to waive it.

Q: Has the prosecutor or anyone else in the District Attorney's office, or the police, or anyone acting under color of authority, threatened you or forced you to testify on your own behalf?

A: No, Sir, no one.

Q: Has your lawyer forced you or given you advice to testify on your own behalf?

A: No, Your Honor, but he did try to talk me out of it.

BY THE COURT: Mr. Public Defender, is this correct?

BY THE PUBLIC DEFENDER: Yes, Your Honor, I advised Mr. Vance against testifying on his own behalf, and told him that if he took the stand, he was doing so against my advice and best judgment.

BY THE COURT: Very well, counsel, you may be seated again. So, Mr. Vance, has anyone promised you leniency, or favorable treatment, or anything else in exchange for your giving testimony on your own behalf?

BY THE DEFENDANT: No, Your Honor, not at all.

Q: Did the D.A. or anyone from the D.A.'s office tell you that you would not get the death penalty if you testified on your own behalf?

A: No, Sir, no one told me anything like this.

Q: So, is your waiver of the privilege against self-incrimination voluntary?

A: Yes, Sir.

Q: And you understand that you are doing this even though it is not required...I mean, even though the Constitution says you are protected against giving testimony that could incriminate you?

A: Yes, Your Honor.

Q: Is it your wish now to give testimony on your own behalf, and to subject yourself to cross-examination by the prosecution?

A: Yes.

Q: ...even though the state has no right to question you or to cross-examine you without this waiver?

A: Yes, Your Honor, I think it would be useful if I testified.

During cross examination, the District Attorney elicited several crucial admissions from Mr. Vance:

BY THE DISTRICT ATTORNEY: So, Mr. Vance, if I hear you right, are you saying that you killed your wife, Stella Vance, in furtherance of a ritual?

BY THE PUBLIC DEFENDER: Your Honor, objection. No foundation, calls for an ultimate conclusion, badgering the witness.

BY THE COURT: Sustained. The jury will disregard the question. Mr. District Attorney, you're treading on thin ice again, and do I need to remind you that this witness is not here to do your job for you. Now rephrase the question or move on.

BY THE DISTRICT ATTORNEY: Yes, Your Honor. Mr. Vance, what is your religion?

BY THE PUBLIC DEFENDER: Your Honor, I'm sorry but I have to object again. This type of question violates the Establishment Clause and is irrelevant to...

BY THE COURT: ...no, counsel, I disagree with you. This question—rather, the answer to this question—may explain things from the defendant's perspective, and it goes to the res gestae, so I'm gonna give the District Attorney some latitude here. But if he strays, I'm gonna rein him back in, don't you worry. The objection is overruled. The State may proceed.

BY THE DISTRICT ATTORNEY: Thank you, Your Honor. Mr. Vance, I'll repeat the question: What is your religion?

BY THE DEFENDANT: I follow the Revelation of Anakum.

Q: Can you explain to the jury what this is?

BY THE PUBLIC DEFENDER: Your Honor, my client has not claimed or been qualified as an expert on theology.

BY THE COURT: Counsel, are you trying to impeach your own client's credibility?

BY THE PUBLIC DEFENDER: No, Your Honor, of course not, it's just that this is not a case about which religion to believe.

BY THE COURT: Well, counsel, I agree with you that the question is vague and overly broad. So, I'll sustain the objection, and the State will rephrase or move on...in double-quick time, got me?

BY THE DISTRICT ATTORNEY: Yes, Your Honor. Mr. Vance, as part of your religion, do you believe in God?

BY THE DEFENDANT: Yes, Sir.

Q: What do you call God in your religion?

A: We don't have to call him anything because he is always there, but we refer to him as a matter of ease or convenience as Tupã.

Q: And does God—or sorry, Tupã as you say—command people who believe in him to do anything?

A: Yes, if you mean are there rules, yes there are rules.

Q: And what are those rules?

A: Promote comfort. Speak truthfully and knowingly. Only ask questions that the person to whom they are posed can answer truthfully and knowingly. Make certain that you never cause blood to spill forth from another being that visibly breathes by inflating and deflating its lungs. And at the beginning of each rainy season, bring the goldsmith all of the gold that you have not given to other Ava, so that he may melt it down and spill it into the river whence it came.

BY THE PUBLIC DEFENDER: Your Honor, I'm not trying to be difficult, but I fail to see the relevance of a theology lesson here, so I'm going to object.

BY THE COURT: Yes, this is going a bit far. Mr. District Attorney, if you're going someplace with this, get there now.

BY THE DISTRICT ATTORNEY: Yes, Sir. Mr. Vance, is correction a rule?

BY THE DEFENDANT: No. It is not a rule. There are only five rules, and I have just told them to you a moment or two ago.

Q: So you did, and I thank you, Mr. Vance. What, then, is correction, if you please.

A: If you do not follow the rules, you must be corrected. That is the example of Anakum.

Q: Where does it say that?

A: In the Revelation itself. "Therefore, on that day, he led the young boy, shouting, by his forelock, put his arms around his shoulders and led him to the hearth. I, Anakum, asked the boy if he was in comfort, and he responded 'Yes.' When the boy was kneeling with his nose touching the ground, Pedro Tannar covered the boy's head with the black velvet cloth and began to recite the rule with which the boy had not complied."

BY THE COURT: Mr. Public Defender, shouldn't you be doing something right now?

BY THE PUBLIC DEFENDER: Yes, Sir, I was just getting my notes together. Objection as to relevance or...umm...outside of the scope of cross examination.

BY THE COURT: Sustained. Mr. Vance, that's enough. I think the jury's got the idea. And you, Mr. District Attorney, this is the last stop. Get off the bus now or else.

BY THE DISTRICT ATTORNEY: Mr. Vance, did you murder your wife Stella Vance?

BY THE PUBLIC DEFENDER: Objection, Your Honor, objection.

BY THE COURT: Sustained. I've just about had it with your antics. The defendant need not answer the question, and the jury will disregard the question.

BY THE DEFENDANT: I don't mind, Your Honor. I corrected Stella because she violated the rules.

BY THE DISTRICT ATTORNEY: Mr. Vance, did you kill her?

A: Well, yes, after the third blow, she was not breathing.

Q: Did you intend to kill her?

BY THE PUBLIC DEFENDER: Objection.

BY THE COURT: Sustained.

BY THE DISTRICT ATTORNEY: May I rephrase?

BY THE COURT: Yes, you'd better.

BY THE DISTRICT ATTORNEY: Mr. Vance, did you intend to hit your wife with...

A: ...Sir, I intended to correct her, and I did correct her.

The twelve-person jury deliberated for three hours, and at 12:30 p.m. on Friday, March 22, 1996, they announced their unanimous verdict finding Mr. Vance guilty of first-degree murder under section 14:30(A)(7) of the Louisiana Revised Statutes.

Under Louisiana law, all trials of capital crimes are bifurcated; thus, only in the event that a guilty verdict is returned does the jury hear evidence and deliberate on the penalty. Accordingly, Judge McCarthy ordered the jury to remain under sequestration and scheduled the penalty phase of the trial to begin three days later at 10:00 a.m.

The State examined the victim's two sisters, as well as her father. None were cross-examined. Though the defense's witness list included ten names, including Mr. Vance's swimming coach, his Latin teacher, his grade-school principal and the priest who had officiated at his marriage to Stella, only Mr. Vance's mother testified in what even the trial court, at the post-conviction phase, characterized "a potentially lethal combination of lukewarm maternal instincts and subliminal accusation":

BY THE PUBLIC DEFENDER: Do you have anything else you'd like to say to the members of the jury to spare your son's life?

BY MRS. EDNA VANCE: Well, I know that we all sure are sorry that things had to end this way. But things are as they are, and we just all have to put our lives in God's hands...(witness makes sobbing noises)... I miss my son, but I miss her too, you know. I'm grieving for Stella 'cause she was a sweet girl and a fantastic mother to those three children.

Judge McCarthy at the trial court instructed the jury at length on the meaning of the various aggravating circumstances that might lead them to impose a death sentence, and explained that even if they decided that one or all of the aggravating circumstances existed beyond a reasonable doubt, they, the jury, could still impose a sentence of life imprisonment without benefit of parole, probation or suspension of sentence. Neither Mr. Vance nor the District Attorney objected to the instructions. The jury deliberated for twenty-eight minutes, and in accordance with article 905.4(A)(7) of the Louisiana Code of Criminal Procedure, found that the killing of Stella Vance had been committed "in an especially heinous, atrocious or cruel manner" which justified their recommending the ultimate penalty of death by lethal injection. Judge McCarthy announced the jury's verdict, ordered Mr. Vance to be placed in the custody of the Louisiana State Penitentiary, and stated on the record that no warrant of execution would be signed until Mr. Vance had exhausted his automatic right of direct appeal to the Louisiana Supreme Court. He adjourned the trial with the following words:

BY THE COURT: I wish you good luck, Mr. Vance. I wish for your sake that things had turned out differently. You're well spoken and young, obviously a smart man with lots of potential. But, you have many different ways to appeal the results reached here today, and I advise you to take full advantage of all of those, and of post-conviction relief as well. All I can say to you at this point is Godspeed.

BY THE DEFENDANT: Thank you, Sir.

The Louisiana Supreme Court, in a per curiam decision, affirmed Mr. Vance's conviction as to both guilt and penalty, and this Court denied Mr. Vance's petition for a writ of certiorari.

The trial court issued a warrant setting Mr. Vance's execution for July 31, 1997. Several days earlier, Mr. Vance's new *pro bono* attorneys, Professor Dylan Hardwick of Loyola Law School and Andrew Sear, both members in good standing of the Louisiana State Bar Association, filed an emergency motion to enroll as counsel and to seek a stay of execution, which the Louisiana Supreme Court granted on the same day.

Through his new counsel, Mr. Vance, on October 31, 1997, returned to the same division of the Orleans Parish Criminal District Court where he was convicted to file a comprehensive application for post-conviction relief pursuant to articles 924 through 930.8 of the Louisiana Code of Criminal Procedure. In this application, Mr. Vance alleged a potpourri of constitutional infirmities requiring the reversal of the jury's verdict on guilt and penalty, focusing on violations of the Establishment and Free Exercise clauses of the First Amendment, as well as denial of federal due process under the Fifth Amendment, ineffective assistance of counsel under the Sixth Amendment, subjection to a cruel and unusual punishment under the Eighth Amendment, and denial of state due process under the Fourteenth Amendment of the United States Constitution.

The trial court, presided again by The Honorable Judge Patrick McCarthy, after hearing extensive oral arguments from both Mr. Vance and the District Attorney, took the matter under advisement. In a written judgment rendered slightly more than a year later, the trial court dismissed all claims except those arising under the First Amendment as made binding on the states through the Fourteenth Amendment, and scheduled an evidentiary hearing on those issues.

Eight months after the completion of the evidentiary hearing, the trial court dismissed Mr. Vance's First Amendment claims, concluding in an eloquent opinion that the Louisiana statute defining first-degree murder as the intentional killing of a human being in furtherance of a "ceremony, rite, initiation, observance, performance or practice" is a "generally applicable, religion-neutral law with the incidental effect of burdening a religious practice of the Anakumists for which the State of Louisiana need not, under *Employment Division v. Smith*, 494 U.S. 872 (1990), put forward any compelling governmental interest."

Mr. Vance appealed to the Louisiana Supreme Court, which affirmed the trial court's judgment of dismissal.

Pursuant to the Antiterrorism and Effective Death Penalty Act of 1996, codified in section 2254 of title 28 of the United States Code, Mr. Vance filed a timely petition for federal post-conviction relief with the United States District Court for the Eastern District of Louisiana. Although the matter had been assigned first to Judge Jonas Hyman, he recused himself on the grounds of a perceived conflict of interest. The Clerk of Court accordingly reallotted the matter to Judge Linda Bonaventure, who dismissed Mr. Vance's petition for post-conviction relief on essentially the same grounds that the Louisiana trial court had assigned in its opinion.

The Court of Appeals for the Fifth Circuit affirmed the dismissal, and Mr. Vance filed a petition for a writ of certiorari with this Court.

We granted certiorari to decide whether the Louisiana statute defining first-degree murder as the killing of a human being when the offender has the specific intent to kill and is engaged in the ritualistic mutilation, dismemberment or torture of a human "as part of a ceremony, rite, initiation, observance, performance or practice" violates the Establishment and Free Exercise Clauses of the United States Constitution.

Law and Analysis

I. STANDARD OF REVIEW

Since this Court's decision in *Everson v. Board of Education*, 330 U.S. 1 (1947), we have held consistently that the Establishment and Free Exercise clauses of the First Amendment confer a fundamental right—that is, a right "implicit in the concept of ordered liberty"—on the citizens of all states. *Palko v. Connecticut*, 302 U.S. 319, 325 (1937). Any state law impacting this fundamental right is subject to "strict scrutiny." *Larson v. Valente*, 456 U.S. 228, 246 (1982). Therefore, this Court must apply "strict scrutiny" to determine whether the Louisiana first-degree murder statute at issue offends the Constitution. *Lukumi Babalu Aye v. City of Hialeah*, 508 U.S. 520, 531-32 (1993). To withstand "strict scrutiny," the state law must be "justified by a compelling governmental interest, and must be narrowly tailored to advance that interest." *Id.*

II. THE ESTABLISHMENT CLAUSE

The First Amendment of the Constitution mandates that "Congress shall make no law respecting an establishment of religion[.]" Because the Fourteenth Amendment prohibits the states from depriving "any person of life, liberty or property, without due process of law," the individual states are as "incompetent as Congress to enact" laws that violate the First Amendment. *Abingdon School Dist. v. Schempp*, 374 U.S. 203, 215-16 (1963) (quoting *Cantwell v. Connecticut*, 310 U.S. 296, 303 (1940)). Thus, it is proper for this Court to consider whether the Louisiana first-degree murder statute violates the Establishment and Free Exercise clauses of the First Amendment.

Literally, the Establishment Clause forbids the government from setting up a church, or from preferring one religion over another. To borrow the words of Thomas Jefferson, the clause was intended to erect "a wall of separation between Church and State." *Everson*, 330 U.S. at 16. This Court has held time and again that this "wall must be kept high and impregnable." *Id.* at 18. Thus, our jurisprudence from the outset has emphasized that neither a state nor the Federal government "can force or influence a person to go to or to remain away from church against his will or force him to profess a belief or disbelief in any religion." *Id.* at 15. Likewise, "[n]o person can be punished for entertaining or professing religious beliefs or disbeliefs[.]" *Id.* at 15-16. In short, the state, especially in the laws it enacts, must be "neutral" towards religion. *Committee for Pub. Educ. & Religious Liberty v. Nyquist*, 413 U.S. 756, 792-93 (1973).

To evaluate the neutrality of a state statute vis-à-vis religion, this Court has adopted a three-pronged inquiry which periodically is criticized by certain of our brethren currently sitting on this Court but which, nonetheless, remains the only binding litmus test: "First, the statute must have a secular legislative purpose; second, its primary or principal effect must be one that neither advances nor inhibits religion, finally, the statute must not foster 'an excessive entanglement with religion.'" *Lemon v. Kurtzman*, 403 U.S. 602, 612-13 (1971) (citations omitted). A statute is unconstitutional if it violates even one of these three prongs. *County of Allegheny v. ACLU, Greater Pittsburgh Chapter*, 492 U.S. 573, 620-21 (1989). Therefore, to determine whether Louisiana's first-degree murder statute runs afoul of the Constitution, we must submit it to the three-pronged *Lemon* test and strictly scrutinize the results.

The first prong requires that the statute under attack have a secular legislative purpose. As one of our own brethren has pointed out on many occasions, any exegesis of a statute's legislative history with a view to divining the intent or purpose of a statute is necessarily a useless endeavor. *See, e.g., Edwards v. Aguillard*, 482 U.S. 578, 636-39 *passim* (1987) (Scalia, J., dissenting). Rather, "[t]he starting point in every case involving construction of a statute is the language itself." *Id.* at 597-98 (Powell, J., concurring in the judgment) (citations omitted). We reaffirm this principle but feel, nonetheless, that a bit of history in the case of this particular statute reveals much.

In 1989—when, according to the testimony of the state's theology expert, Anakumism began to experience a "phenomenal wave of expansion in the United States and the Middle East"—the Louisiana legislature criminalized "ritualistic acts" and "ritualistic mutilation, dismemberment, or torture of a human[,]" recognizing that "the people of Louisiana [are] grateful to Almighty God for the civil, political, economic and religious liberties we enjoy," and expressly finding "that this enactment is *necessary* for the *immediate* preservation of the public peace, health, morals, safety, and welfare and for the support of state government and its public institutions." LA. REV. STAT. ANN. § 14:107.1 (emphasis added). The same statute also defines "ritualistic acts" as "those acts undertaken as part of a ceremony, rite, initiation, observance, performance, or practice that result in or are intended to result in...[t]he mutilation, dismemberment, torture, abuse of sacrifice of animals [or the] ingestion of human or animal blood or human or animal waste." We struck down a similar Florida ordinance as an unconstitutional burden on the free exercise of the Santeria religion in *Lukumi Babalu Aye*, 508 U.S. at 547.

Under the 1989 enactment, the penalty for committing a "ritualistic act" on an animal is a maximum of five years' imprisonment or a fine of $5,000, or both. For a "ritualistic mutilation" of a human, the penalty is five times greater: twenty-five years' imprisonment or $25,000, or both. In both cases, the crimes are misdemeanors.

Section 14:107(C) offers no definition of "ritualistic mutilation, dismemberment, or torture of a human." However, in the same act by which it criminalized ritualistic acts and mutilations, the Louisiana legislature amended another statute, section 14:30, to define as first-degree murder any killing of a human where the offender had specific intent to kill and committed an act prohibited by section 14:107(C)(1)—that is, any "*ritualistic* mutilation, dismemberment or torture of a human as part of a *ceremony, rite, initiation, observance, performance or practice*" (emphasis added). Notably, this is the only statute under which Mr. Vance was charged, prosecuted and convicted.

The crucial question is whether this first-degree murder statute has a non-secular legislative purpose. The official statement of legislative purpose contained within section 14:107(A)(1) is nothing more than a generic, albeit somewhat exaggerated, justification of the state's exercise of its police power. This may be sufficient to justify economic legislation, but not to satisfy strict scrutiny where a fundamental right—such as the freedom of religion enshrined within the First Amendment—is burdened. *See United States v. Carolene Products Co.*, 304 U.S. 144, 152 n.4 (1938). In the case of a state law that is clear on its face—as the Louisiana first-degree murder statute is—"a fundamental canon of statutory interpretation is that, unless otherwise defined, words will be interpreted as taking their ordinary, contemporary, common meaning." *Perrin v. United States*, 444 U.S. 37, 42 (1979). Of course, the word "religious" is nowhere found in the statute, but "ritual" relates to "the order of words prescribed for a *religious* ceremony" or a "system of rites." WEBSTER'S NEW COLLEGIATE DICTIONARY 1000 (1975) (emphasis added). This plain meaning is confirmed by a comparison of this dictionary definition with the legislature's definition of "ritualistic act"—a "ceremony, rite, or sacrifice" where animals are mutilated or human or animal blood is ingested. The use of the words "sacrifice" and "ritual" in a statute are "consistent with [a] claim of facial discrimination." *Lukumi Babalu Aye*, 508 U.S. at 533-34. In the *Lukumi* case, the municipal lawmakers of Hialeah did not modify "mutilation" with the adjective "ritualistic." How much more offensive is the Louisiana statute, which requires that the mutilation be "ritualistic" *and* "part of a ceremony, rite, or practice"? Therefore, we conclude that the word "ritualistic" is merely a euphemism for "religious"—and given the spread of this faith and its practices in Louisiana, maybe even for "Anakumist."

The presence of this adjective in the Louisiana statute cannot be dismissed as surplusage, for this Court always presumes that state legislators know and intend what they write.

In any event, "discerning the subjective motivation of those enacting the statute is, to be honest, almost always an impossible task. To look for the sole purpose of even a single legislator is probably to look for something that does not exist." *Edwards*, 482 U.S. at 637 (Scalia, J., dissenting). Hence, in conducting the first *Lemon* inquiry, we scour "the face of the statute"—not the legislative history or the debate transcripts—for "a *plausible* secular purpose." *Mueller v. Allen*, 463 U.S. 388, 394-95 (1983) (emphasis added).

We need not engage in Byzantine exegesis. On the face of this statute, the State of Louisiana could not have successfully convicted Mr. Vance of first-degree murder had he merely killed his wife with three blows of a *molcajete* to the skull; this would be, at best, second-degree murder. Only when the state introduced expert *theological* testimony on the importance of correction to practitioners of the Anakumist religion—evidence that, by the way, Mr. Vance's own testimony confirmed—could it discharge its burden of proving the elements of first-degree murder under section 14:30(A)(7). And lest anyone trivialize the chasm between the two degrees of murder in Louisiana, first-degree murderers can be sentenced to death, whereas those convicted of second-degree murder cannot. This bears repeating: Under the Louisiana statute, only ritualistic (i.e., religious) mutilators who kill their victims may be executed; secular mutilators face a maximum term of life imprisonment. How much less secular can the Louisiana legislature have been?

This Court is well aware of the prejudice and persecution to which the Anakumists have been subjected not only in the United States, but worldwide. This fact, however, does not motivate our decision here. Even if we concede that the state had a compelling purpose for criminalizing "ritualistic acts" and "ritualistic mutilations," we fail to see how singling out religious mutilations from all others is "necessary" to serve this end. A much less restrictive alternative exists: The Louisiana statute could define every perpetrator of a human "mutilation, dismemberment or torture" resulting in death as a first-degree murderer. Then the statute would have no constitutional infirmity, and Mr. Vance would have no grounds to challenge his conviction or sentence. However, as soon as the state distinguishes a "ritualistic"—that is, religious—killing from an intentional murder committed for secular reasons (e.g., a Republican Mafia *capo* plucking out the tongue of a Democrat, thereby causing his death by exsanguination) by making only the religious crimes eligible for the death penalty, it is expressly singling out religion, thereby betraying—even if unwittingly—a non-secular purpose and breaching Jefferson's wall of separation between Church and State. Accordingly, the statute fails the first prong of the *Lemon* test.

Our learned brother Justice C.D., joined by our learned brother Justice E.F., notes in his concurrence that Mr. Vance's crime could not constitute a "ritualistic mutilation" committed in furtherance of a religious practice because Anakumism is not a religion, but "at best a pseudo-revolutionary political or social movement appealing to, and deriving its steam from, Generation X's obsession with obscenity, sodomy, homosexual and bisexual fellatio and intercourse, polygamy, *ménages à trois*, and an otherwise morally bankrupt and devil-may-care world outlook." Here, however, our concurring brethren are drawing their own emotionally-driven inferences from facts not contained within the transcript of the trial or the post-conviction pleadings. Throughout his voluntary testimony, Mr. Vance repeatedly referred to Anakumism as a religion, and the District Attorney never interposed a single objection. Moreover, at trial, the state called a distinguished theologian from Harvard Divinity School to testify on the majority and minority views among Anakumists on the appropriateness and applicability of correction in the modern world, and he was qualified as an expert without objection by Mr. Vance's trial attorney. Therefore, with all due respect to our learned brethren, the issue of whether Anakumism is a religion *vel non* has been fully adjudicated in a proper adversarial forum and is not properly before this Court, which we repeatedly have held is without jurisdiction to render advisory opinions or to make rulings *sua sponte*.

Even though the Louisiana statute has failed one prong of the *Lemon* test and is therefore unconstitutional, we proceed to the second prong which "is useful because of the analytic content it gives to the *Lemon*-mandated inquiry into legislative purpose and effect." *Wallace v. Jaffree*, 472 U.S. 38, 70 (1985) (O'Connor, J., concurring in the judgment). To pass this second test, the statute must be "neutral towards religion." *Schempp*, 374 U.S. at 222.

At the risk of reiterating the glaringly obvious, this statute is not neutral towards religion, but expressly targets it. "Rite" and "ceremony" are words from the lexicon of religion, and both are present in the statute *sub judice*. Perhaps our dissenting and concurring brethren will be convinced by the following hypothesis: Suppose that a newlywed dices his young wife up into small, bite-size pieces and stir-fries her for dinner because he likes the taste of human flesh. Under Louisiana's murder statute, he is not guilty of first-degree murder, but at most of second-degree murder, and if convicted, will spend the rest of his life in prison (barring a pardon). If, however, the state proves beyond a reasonable doubt that the young husband killed his wife as a human sacrifice to Satan, Kali, Huizilopochtli, Inti, or Pachamama, or as the result of an Anakumist correction rite, the crime is converted into first-degree murder, and if convicted, the husband can, at the jury's sole discretion, be put to death. In sum, the first-degree murder statute targets religion and, thus, fails the second prong of the *Lemon* test.

The third and final prong under *Lemon* is whether the statute under attack fosters "excessive entanglement" between the state and religion. We recognize that this entanglement cannot be gauged with scientific precision. *Roemer v. Maryland Pub. Works Bd.*, 426 U.S. 736, 766 (1976). It is clear, though, that if the enforcement of a statute requires a state to verify which activities are secular and which are religious, the entanglement is excessive. *See, e.g., Levitt v. Committee for Pub. Educ. & Religious Liberty*, 413 U.S. 472, 480 (1973).

In order to prosecute a defendant under this first-degree murder statute, the district attorneys in Louisiana must investigate whether the mutilations were "ritualistic" and committed as part of a "rite" or "ceremony." They must, therefore, inquire into the contents of others' religious beliefs to properly classify the murder as first-degree or second-degree. At trial, to convict the defendant and have the chance of putting him to death, the state will have to introduce—and pay with state funds for—theological experts to testify on the question of whether the killing indeed was "ritualistic." Judges and jurors alike will have to base their decisions on the testimony of such theologians, all the while struggling with the all-too-human temptation of approving or disapproving of religious practices simply as a matter of conscience or prejudice. This divisive struggle—which forced the founders of this country to seek asylum in the New World—is clearly the evil that the drafters of the Establishment Clause sought to avoid. By obliging the state to consider religious questions when charging or prosecuting a defendant under section 14:30(A)(7), the Louisiana "ritualistic murder" statute fosters excessive entanglement. Thus, the third prong of *Lemon* is not satisfied.

Because we find that the first-degree murder statute under which Mr. Vance was convicted and sentenced fails all three prongs of the *Lemon* test , it violates the Establishment Clause of the First Amendment to the United States Constitution.

III. THE FREE EXERCISE CLAUSE

Although the Louisiana "ritualistic murder" statute is unconstitutional under the Establishment Clause, we proceed to dispose of Mr. Vance's remaining claim. Like the Establishment Clause, the Free Exercise Clause binds not only the Federal government, but the states as well. *Abingdon, supra*, 374 U.S. at 215-16. It protects "first and foremost, the right to believe and profess whatever religious doctrine one desires." *Employment Division, supra*, 494 U.S. at 877. The religious beliefs "need not be acceptable, logical, consistent or comprehensible to others in order to merit First Amendment protection." *Thomas v. Review Bd. of Indiana Employment Security Div.*, 450 U.S. 707, 714 (1981). Moreover, the Free Exercise Clause "protect[s] religious observers against unequal treatment." *Hobbie v. Unemployment Appeals Comm'n of Fla.*, 480 U.S. 136, 148 (1987) (Stevens, J., concurring in judgment). Consequently, any law targeting "religious beliefs as such is never permissible." *McDaniel v. Paty*, 435 U.S. 618, 626 (1978). On the other hand, "if prohibiting the exercise of religion is not the object of the [law] but merely the incidental effect of a generally applicable and otherwise valid provision," the state has not violated the Free Exercise Clause. *Employment Division*, 494 U.S. at 878 (citations omitted).

The threshold inquiry, then, is whether the ritualistic murder statute is "generally applicable." The District Attorney, in his oral argument, stated that the purpose of the statute was to deter "cruel and depraved murders committed by means of torture and mutilation." That, however, is not how the statute is written. If the District Attorney is to be taken at his word, the statute is under-inclusive for it exposes to the death penalty only those offenders who commit "ritualistic" murders "as part of a ceremony, rite, or practice." All others who commit murder through non-ritualistic mutilation or for non-ritualistic reasons—that is, through secular mutilation or torture (e.g., a racist white man chops the hands and feet off his black neighbor)—are guilty of second-degree murder, and face a maximum sentence of life imprisonment. Such under-inclusiveness on the face of the statute is indicative of the "precise evil" that "the requirement of general applicability is designed to prevent." *Lukumi Babalu Aye*, 508 U.S. at 545-46.

The Free Exercise Clause "forbids [even] subtle departures from neutrality." *Gillette v. United States*, 401 U.S. 437, 452 (1971). Thus, this Court "must survey meticulously the circumstances of governmental categories to eliminate, as it were, religious gerrymanders." *Walz v. Tax Comm'n of New York City*, 397 U.S. 664, 696 (1970) (Harlan, J., concurring). In the Louisiana criminal statutes, there are two categories: first-degree murder for murders committed through ritualistic mutilations as part of a ceremony or rite, and second-degree murder for all other murders by mutilation. The distinction between the two degrees is literally a question of life or death. This is the quintessence of religious gerrymandering, and a "law that targets religious conduct for distinctive treatment will survive strict scrutiny only in rare cases." *Lukumi Babalu Aye*, 508 U.S. at 545. This, alas, is not one of those cases, for the State of Louisiana could have tailored the statute to prevent, in the District Attorney's words, "cruel and depraved murders through torture and mutilation" by simply deleting the word "ritualistic." The failure of the Louisiana legislature to tailor narrowly the first-degree statute to combat the evil it sought to address is by itself sufficient to establish the statute's unconstitutionality. *See Arkansas Writers' Project, Inc. v. Ragland*, 481 U.S. 221, 232 (1987).

Our learned brother Justice G.H. in his dissent expresses his belief that this statute passes constitutional muster because it applies also to "drunken fraternity brothers who make their pledges copulate with sheep and eat live scorpions." This logic is facetious, for to this Court's knowledge, no fraternity member engages in initiations with the specific intent of killing a pledge. In fact, it bears mentioning here something that we have not raised up to this point: Of Louisiana's seven categories of first-degree murder, only the "ritualistic mutilation" murder requires that the offender have "specific intent to kill" instead of "specific intent to kill or inflict great bodily harm." We presume that this is not an example of inept or sloppy drafting, but rather constitutes further evidence that in passing this first-degree murder statute, the legislature was specifically targeting the Anakumist practice of correction.

In closing, we reiterate what we have already written elsewhere: "Those in office must be resolute in resisting importunate demands and must ensure that the sole reasons for imposing the burdens of law and regulation are secular. Legislators may not devise mechanisms, overt or disguised, designed to persecute or oppress a religion or its practices." *Lukumi Babalu Aye*, 508 U.S. at 547. The Louisiana statute defining as first-degree murder any specific-intent killing resulting from "ritualistic mutilation as part of a ceremony, rite, initiation, observance, performance, or practice" violates the Establishment and Free Exercise Clauses of the First Amendment to the United States Constitution and, therefore, is void.

For the foregoing reasons, this Court holds that the judgment of the Fifth Circuit Court of Appeals affirming Mr. Ed Vance's conviction and death sentence is reversed. The State of Louisiana has thirty days to initiate proceedings against Mr. Vance under another, valid statute, and if it fails to act within that time, the Warden of the Louisiana State Penitentiary is hereby ordered to release Mr. Vance from his custody.

JUSTICE C.D., joined by JUSTICE E.F., concurring in the judgment only.

I concur fully in the judgment reached by the majority that Mr. Vance's conviction and penalty must be reversed. However, I write separately because I reach this result via a route that my brothers and sisters on the Court simply bypassed.

The Louisiana statute *sub judice*, section 14:30(A)(7), defines first-degree murder as the killing of a human being where the perpetrator had specific intent to kill and committed a "*ritualistic* mutilation as part of a ceremony, rite, or practice" (emphasis added). I agree with the majority's interpretation that the term "ritualistic mutilation," particularly when combined with the words "as part of a ceremony, rite, or practice," compels the conclusion that the legislature was targeting religious rather than secular acts. However, I am not at all prepared to follow the State, Mr. Vance and the majority of this Court in glibly conceding that Anakumism is a religion.

One of the elements of the crime—indeed, the spool around which the thread of the majority's entire legal argument is wound—is that the mutilation must be "ritualistic." Another necessary element is that the crime must be committed "as part of a ceremony, rite, or practice." As two distinct elements of the offense, these are legal questions, not factual ones, and thus—contrary to the majority's critique of this concurrence—this Court is not bound by the record, by Mr. Vance's confession or, much less, by the State of Louisiana's subjective characterization of Anakumism as a religion.

I have found nothing in the recent English translation of *The Revelation of Anakum* (Singapore: World Anakumist League, 1992) to suggest that the majority's *ipse dixit* is correct. What I have found, instead of an inspired scripture or a divine revelation, is a diary of the most repulsively graphic pornography, a glorification of homosexuality, and a call to arms against the rich. Indeed, in a recent presidential campaign in Argentina, one of the underdog candidates adopted as his slogan *Acúdanse a la quinta*, "come down to the ranch," which could also be translated "come down to the fifth"—a veiled reference, say a number of commentators, to Anakum's fifth rule: "At the beginning of each rainy season, bring the goldsmith all of the gold that you have not given to other Ava, so that he may melt it down and spill it into the river whence it came." (Citations omitted). Various commentators have suggested that this movement is responsible for provoking the recent wave of violence in the Middle East. Does this sound like a religion?

Anakumism cannot be a religion because it ordains no clergy, builds no churches or temples, maintains no hierarchy, and prescribes no liturgy. It is at best a pseudo-revolutionary political or social movement appealing to, and deriving its steam from, Generation X's obsession with obscenity, sodomy, homosexual and bisexual fellatio and intercourse, polygamy, *ménages à trois*, and an otherwise morally bankrupt and devil-may-care world outlook. As we have repeatedly held, it is well-established law that none of these activities implicate fundamental rights. *See, e.g., Bowers v. Hardwick*, 478 U.S. 186 (1986) (consensual homosexual sodomy not entitled to constitutional protection),[1] *Miller v.*

---

[1] ★ ★ Author's Note: The Supreme Court, on June 26, 2003, overturned its own decision in *Bowers*, recognizing that persons engaging in consensual homosexual intercourse have a "right to liberty under the Due Process Clause [which] gives them the full right to

California, 413 U.S. 15 (1973) (obscenity not protected under the First Amendment), *Reynolds v. United States*, 98 U.S. 145 (1879) (Mormons not entitled to practice polygamy). Whatever the nature of the right Mr. Vance is asking this Court to recognize, he is certainly not entitled to seek the umbrage of the Establishment or Free Exercise Clause because Anakumism is no more a religion than Communism. As a matter of fact, then, I would find that Anakumism is not a religion, and this would lead me to hold as a matter of law that the mutilation of Stella Vance by her husband could not have been "ritualistic" *and* "part of a ceremony, rite, or practice." For these reasons, and not those suggested by the majority, the State of Louisiana has not proven the elements of first-degree murder under section 14:30(A)(7).

I am of course somewhat reluctant to reverse Mr. Vance's conviction and sentence because, in so doing, I may well be setting a cold-blooded murderer free. However, in the global scheme, this is by far the lesser of two evils. For if I assume with the majority that Anakumism is a bona fide religion—and I apologize for these *obiter dicta*—it is only a matter of time before this Court will come face-to-face with the issue of a tax exemption for some of the multibillion dollar real-estate holdings that the Anakumists, according to the Harvard religious expert's testimony at Mr. Vance's trial, have amassed over the past few decades in New York, New Orleans and Las Vegas, and the proponent will cite the relevant portion of the majority's opinion here as binding precedent for the proposition that Anakumism is indeed a religion. Accordingly, this Court may well find its hands tied, and this, quite simply, I am unwilling to countenance.

Let the judgment of this Court today sound a message to prosecutors in Louisiana and throughout this country: to

---

engage in their conduct without intervention of the government."
Lawrence v. Texas, 539 U.S. 558, 578 (2003).

quote a maxim from the world of tax planning, "pigs get fat, but hogs get slaughtered." Had the State of Louisiana simply charged and prosecuted Mr. Vance on the lesser-included offense of second-degree murder, any jury in the state would have convicted him on the basis of his trial testimony alone, and Mr. Vance would be spending the rest of his natural life at hard labor in a maximum-security prison. Or the District Attorney could have chosen not to drop the two counts of possession with intent to distribute coca leaves, each of which, under Louisiana's version of the Uniform Controlled Substance Act, constitutes a felony punishable by mandatory imprisonment for a minimum of five and not more than thirty years, in addition to a fine ranging from $50,000 to $150,000.

However, in his greed or political ambition or both, the District Attorney focused all of his energy on chalking up another death-penalty conviction, as evidenced by his emotional closing statements and crocodile tears in both the guilt and penalty phases of the trial. As if following the script of a classical tragedy, the District Attorney gambled and lost through his hubris, but he cannot expect this Court now to drop onto the scene like some *deus ex machina* to pick up the pieces. That the electorate will have to do.

Because the State has failed to discharge its burden by proving beyond a reasonable doubt the elements of first-degree murder contained in section 14:30(A)(7), I concur in the Court's judgment reversing Mr. Vance's conviction and sentence.

JUSTICE G.H., dissenting.

I do not dare be as presumptuous as the majority to run roughshod over the prior decisions of this Court. The first-degree murder statute in question has the secular purpose and effect of punishing cold-blooded murderers. Moreover, it is a generally applicable law, not an impermissible burden on a benign religious practice. Yes, the statute applies to Anakumists engaging in correction, as it does to crazed rabbis who cut off more than the foreskin and frustrated priests who drown infants in the baptismal font, not to mention drunken fraternity brothers who make their pledges copulate with sheep and eat live scorpions. Are we now to hold as a matter of law that fraternities are entitled to seek refuge under the Establishment and Free Exercise Clauses of the Constitution?

Killing cannot be cloaked with respectability simply by being labeled the crucial practice of some esoteric new religion. I see no constitutional violation under either pertinent clause of the First Amendment, no matter how wide its umbrella might be.

Accordingly, I would affirm Mr. Vance's conviction as well as the death sentence imposed on him after a full and fair hearing by a jury of his peers.

POSTSCRIPT

POSTSCRIPT

On the twenty-ninth day, just before lunch, the District Attorney of Orleans Parish strolled into a press room bulging with cameras, lights and journalists. He was not ranting and raving as usual, but wearing a faint smile that actually made him appear, for a second, to have recaptured the innocence of his days as star captain of the Jesuit High School football team. Sporting a new summer suit that he might even have purchased from Ed Vance's father's haberdashery, he radiated the composure and look of an incumbent bidding for a reelection he was assured of winning.

He positioned himself nervously at the podium and took a folded sheet out of his breast pocket. "Ladies and gentlemen, I only have a short statement for y'all today. The big boys in Washington overturned the first-degree murder statute that Ed Vance was convicted under, and gave us until tomorrow to release him from custody or initiate a proceeding against him under another statute."

One could have heard a pin drop, save for the bulbs that flashed like a nearby lightning strike. The District Attorney folded up the paper, adjusted his tie and grinned more broadly for the television audience.

"At this point, we feel it would be useless to retry Mr. Vance. Thank you."

✳

The story is supposed to end there, but stories like Anakum's and Ed Vance's do not end where they ought to end. They send out tentacles and roots, some so fine that you do not see them until you are tangled up within them.

When I was a child, my grandmother used to say that nothing ever stays the same, not even misfortune or bad luck, but for things to change, you simply need to be at the right place at the right time. As time went on, I realized that common-sensical though this piece of folk wisdom was, it was not correct. In fact, for the tectonic plates supporting the status quo to shift, one had to steel oneself to live through the unpredictability of an earthquake. Perhaps one would emerge only with minor scratches, perhaps one would be buried alive beneath a city of rubble. In other words, for revolutionary change to occur to an individual, he had to be at the wrong place at the right time, or the right place at the wrong time. Whichever way it turns out, it is not going to be clean and sanitary; one is bound to get dirty, no matter how hard one resolves to keep one's head above the dust.

In my wildest fantasies—and God, I have had more than I could ever count—I never imagined that I would be looking over my shoulders, trying to pick out the all-too-obvious signs of a professional shadow. Who on Earth could possibly be interested in knowing where I was going, whom I was meeting, what I was writing? But, it is not pure coincidence when the same guy with Ray-Bans and earphones comes into Starbuck's on the Jeddah corniche five minutes after you whenever you happen to be in the mood for a decaf Americano or check out the "local produce," is it?

My first hint that I was being trailed came when I was visiting my mother in New York. Whenever I picked up her landline and dialed a number, there was a delay of several seconds. I asked her whether she had ever noticed this, but she shook her head: "The phone hardly ever rings except when you happen to be here."

When I started perceiving a click, it was extremely faint at first, like someone down the hall was crumbling a piece of newspaper every few seconds. At first, that only happened when I was back in town, until I noticed that I would hear the same crinkling on the line whenever I would call my mother from Saudi Arabia or Oman. After three or four years out of the country, I became so scandalized by the static on my telephone line that I stopped using the home phone altogether and exclusively used a prepaid phone chip which, in an abundance of caution, I changed every four or five weeks.

Then there was the incident of the white Nissan following me back to my apartment every day at 8:45 p.m. My route was hardly direct: my apartment was on the ground floor of a nondescript building on a small cul-de-sac in a working-class neighborhood behind the Firestone headquarters on Palestine Road. To reach it from my office in Rawdah, I had to make a total of eight left turns and four right ones, some onto alleyways so narrow that they had to have been planned before the advent of the automobile. A Nissan could barely pass through, especially if men were streaming out of the mosque. I went down that particular alleyway, from which I had to make a very sharp right into heavy traffic, expressly to avoid tails. Mr. Nissan, though, was a determined sort, and though he lost me a few times as I made that sharp right turn, he invariably found me.

One particularly scary night, I noticed him park his white Nissan in front of the apartment building next to mine. He sat behind the wheel for hours, smoking a cigarette, listening to a cassette tape of Umm Kalthoum. He occasionally looked with expectation toward my window or my Caprice. At 10:45, he got out of the car and approached the front steps of my building. He studied the number plate on the building—nobody pays attention to them except electricity meter readers and Pizza Hut delivery boys—then disappeared into the darkness beyond my peripheral vision. I myself disappeared into the *majlis*, humming the last song he had been listening to with the car window wide open, *Al Atlal*.

Then the doorbell rang. The sound killed the tune in my head and pierced my chest. My heart began to thump uncontrollably. My face flushed. I began to sweat.

I pushed my Ethiopian houseboy towards the door and told him to find out who this strange man was and what he wanted. I could not catch my breath. I tried to swallow, but my tongue was paralyzed and my throat stuffed with cotton. I barely gulped.

"Doctor," my officious Ethiopian called out, "he is looking for a furnished flat."

"A what?"

"He said that he wants to rent a flat for himself, and he wants to speak to the landlord." I grew more suspicious than ever: this Saudi man, whoever he was, must know that I was not the landlord because non-Saudis like me cannot own real estate.

"Get rid of him."

"Just talk to him, Doctor. He is *miskeen.*" "Poor" and "nice": it is one of those wonderful words, of which the Arabic language is full, which can carry seemingly unrelated, even contradictory, meanings. In Omani Arabic, *ta'baan* can mean "tired," "sick," "horny," or "sexually passive." What any one speaker intends to say depends entirely on the context.

When I confronted Abdullah, for that was his name, he seemed to have tears pooling at the corners of his eyes, and this, strangely, put me at ease. His hands were clamped together in front of his crotch and trembling. I almost pitied him until my righteous indignation at being followed every day for the last month rose to the surface.

"*As-salamu alaykum wa rahmat Ullah.* What can I do for you?"

"I am looking for a nice apartment with furniture. I am a bachelor. Is this a family accommodation?" In Saudi Arabia, buildings are either for families or bachelors, never for both.

"Yes, it is."

He grew distressed and wiped his forehead. "Oh, I am sorry. I hope Madame is not sleeping. I didn't know..."

"It's ok. She's not here." Because she doesn't exist, I thought. "I'm sorry, Abdullah, this is a family building, and there are no vacancies in any case."

"Well, can I speak to your landlord anyway?"

I pointed up the dark staircase. "Yes, third floor." I knew that my landlord, who had three unmarried daughters living at home, would never open the door to a single Arab male at almost 11 o'clock at night.

The next day at the office, my boss' son Yasir was asking me whether everything was going well in my apartment and whether I might be interested in moving. "You know, that area of Palestine Road is full of Palestinians and low-class Syrians. Scum of the earth." He spit these nationalities out like curses. And so it was that feigning illness, I stayed home the next day and packed a single suitcase. Twenty-four hours thereafter, I was on a Turkish Airlines flight to Istanbul en route to New York to tend to my mother who, like me, had fallen suddenly ill. Halfway over the Atlantic, while munching on hazelnuts and drinking raki, I made up my mind to abandon everything I had left behind in Jeddah: a job, cash, a gold Rolex, a collection of Montblanc fountain pens, and a Chevrolet Caprice that admittedly had seen better days, not to mention an Ethiopian houseboy. I would never return to Saudi Arabia because everything, suddenly, had become clear.

✳

I had not yet overcome the brutal east-to-west jet lag when, the Saturday following my return to Brooklyn, the phone that never rings for my mother did indeed wake me up from a long afternoon nap. I picked up the receiver, dropped it and picked it up again, only to hear the rustling of an unopened bag of potato chips followed by a dull buzzing, like a lone mosquito in a dark bedroom. I slammed the receiver down.

"Ma, when are you going to get the damned phone number changed like I told you?" In retrospect, I realize how naïve I was: Did I really think that changing my mother's number, even delisting it, would prevent *him*, or anyone else, from finding me?

The phone shrilled again. I was fuming. "Yeah, what? Speak!"

The static was gone, at least momentarily. I perceived a human breath, which differs from an animal breath in that there is always a hint of desperation in it.

"Hello, is this the home of David Ball? David Augustus Ball?"

The cocky self-assurance, the intellectual snobbism, whisked me back to the classroom at Loyola where I used to roll my eyes and make rude gestures under the desk whenever he and Professor Hardwick would go off on one of their Socratic debates about the nature of an acceptance by acquiescence. I was not going to give him the satisfaction of being remembered. His Polo shirts with the collars turned up limply, an effect it took hours in front of a mirror to perfect, and his impeccably faded blue jeans used to annoy me, offend me, because he had no right to look good *and* be smart, the smug asshole.

Fuck him.

"Yes it is. Who is this please?"

"David?"

"Yes, with whom am I speaking?" With this urban philosopher, one had to make sure to use the accusative case lest one be castigated for laxity.

"David, this is Andy...Andy Sear from Loyola. I need your help." With fat social misfits like me, who couldn't fit into impeccably faded blue jeans if their lives depended on it, Andy could get right to the point, and he knew it. He knew with whom he could take liberties and for whom he had to abase himself through sycophancy. There was no reason to impress me because he surely knew, even after that mediated reconciliation of sorts at the Kit Kat Klub, that I was eaten alive by envy over his mind and his looks, not to mention his boundless self-confidence.

That initial telephone call did not last long enough for the glacier of resentment and repugnance towards Andy to melt away. Like me, he was wary of the crackling on my mother's telephone line, and he suggested that I meet him on Friday at noon at the counter at the Oyster Bar in Grand Central Terminal, which, it being Lent, would be brimming over with Catholic businessmen and accountants doing penance by abstaining from meat.

I was awfully curious. I was almost ashamed of how much I wanted to see him again, but I had to appear put-upon. "How will I find you? I mean, it's been almost fifteen years, Andy."

"I will find you. Don't you think I remember what you look like, David?" He laughed, but it was more like a cough. "I wasn't that shitfaced at the Kit Kat."

I was actually astonished that he remembered that I even existed.

I was finishing up an oyster pan roast—plump oysters dropped from the shell into a steaming cauldron of cream and cayenne pepper—and looking at my watch every ten seconds or so. "What a fucking mistake! I should have known this douchebag would send me on a wild goose chase." I had just asked the waitress for my check when a hand grasped my right shoulder from directly behind me.

"Hi David. Fancy meeting you here!"

I twirled around on the stool which was a tad too close to the counter for my comfort, but Andy had been insistent on the phone that I not wait for him at the entrance. What awaited me literally took my breath away: gone were the perfectly faded blue jeans and the upturned collar, and in their place stood a chubby, graying, nondescript man with chipmunk jowls that hid the dimples that I used to find so threatening to my sense of self-worth. Instead of a Yankees cap, a natty navy beret was perched sideways on his head (it was particularly chilly that spring), and when he shoved it back so that he could wipe the pearls of sweat from his furrowed brow, I could not help but notice that his once wavy black hair was now much sparser. He grinned, but it was a feigned gesture; to someone looking on from afar, he might have appeared constipated or just on the verge of coming down with a nasty cold.

He spoke quickly and with little punctuation, except what was naturally required to bring the spoon from his bowl of New England clam chowder to his lips. After serving as a federal law clerk, Andy joined forces with our old professor, Dylan Hardwick, who pushed him deeper and deeper into the netherworld of *pro bono* criminal appeals and habeas corpus petitions. That is the time when he was thrust headfirst into the maelstrom of a high-profile murder conviction marred by a First Amendment issue of first impression. This case brought Andy and Professor Hardwick—I, unlike Andy, could never get used to calling him Dylan—all the way to the rarefied corridors of the Supreme Court in Washington.

"How is Professor Hardwick these days?" I asked not out of concern for the perverted narcissist, but because I was struggling to discern just where this unorthodox reunion was heading, and as Professor Hardwick was the only human link between Andy and myself, I figured that the Professor's name might be the appropriate segue.

Andy didn't miss a beat. "Dead." He took another sip of his Bombay Sapphire martini, straight up, shaken not stirred, with two anchovy-stuffed Spanish olives, just as he had ordered it, without even looking over at me to gauge my reaction. "Cirrhosis. Poor guy."

I did not know how to react; I had not been expecting to receive this bit of news. It was no secret, certainly not to Andy, that I did not particularly like or respect Professor Hardwick but, in retrospect, I acknowledge that this antagonism was due principally to my exclusion from his inner sanctum of other pompous, self-aggrandizing drunks who got off on hearing themselves pontificate...drunks like Andy Sear, who looked so barren, gray and...dare I say it?...pathetic. He ordered a third martini just as the lull in the conversation wrapped the noose around my throat and tightened.

"David, do you mind if we go to a table in the bar? It's easier to talk there."

I confess that I was feeling more than a bit annoyed with this cloak-and-dagger attitude of his. Now that lunch was over, why couldn't we just get to the bottom of what it was that required my input after all these years of silence and intentional neglect?

Fortified by his third Bombay Sapphire martini, Andy launched right into the subject without even bothering to look at me or otherwise give me a sign of his earnestness or desperation. "I recall that you are fluent in Guaraní." Oneupmanship at this stage demanded self-deprecation. "I wouldn't say fluent, but I guess I can get along all right for a gringo." I laughed a bit too hard and wished that I had a cocktail to stare into. "I lived in Paraguay for a while during the 80s, and it is damned near impossible to step outside and talk to people if you can't make yourself understood in the language." Did he drag me all this way to have a chat about linguistics?

Andy looked concerned, forlorn. He seemed on the verge of letting out a sigh of disappointment, but instead, he sat straight up in his chair and stared straight into my eyes. I was catatonic. "But if you saw something written in Guaraní, you could pretty much take it apart and get to the bottom of what it said, right?" This was now an interrogation, and I was seized by the urge to escape from that dark-tiled dungeon and breathe some cool air again. "I guess so, Andy, but there's a problem with Guaraní because the orthography has never been standardized. Some still use the Jesuits' antiquated system, while the Paraguayan government has..."

He interrupted me out of impatience rather than anger because the martini with two anchovy-stuffed Spanish olives remained firmly cupped in his hands. "But you could try, right? You feel competent enough to try?"

The moment for humility had passed, but I was not in the mood to do this guy any favors. It was time to start looking out for my own best interests. "Sure, Andy, but...and you'll excuse my...umm...impertinence or brusqueness, but where is all this going?"

He laughed heartily, out loud, probably for the first time in a long while, and spilled a few drops of his precious drink onto his lap. I felt a momentary pang of guilt for being so abrupt. He looked at me and smiled so broadly that I could see his teeth were still pearly white. "I deserved that, I guess."

The story took the better part of three more Bombay Sapphire martinis to tell, and I finally had no choice but to accompany Andy, knowing fully well that I was going to leave the Oyster Bar drunk that evening. The First Amendment murder case that Andy and the late Professor Hardwick took on involved a correction rite of Anakumism, which Andy described as a "a post-Christian revelation meant to ensure that the Gospel, as it has been preached for two thousand years, becomes a living, breathing, all-encompassing way of life." He was more than shocked to hear that I had already heard of Anakumism, and I revealed to him my friendship with Dr. Goma, who had shown me that obscure yellow-bound book about Anakum the new prophet so many years before. He shrugged his shoulders: "I've never heard of Dr. Goma, David, but there are so many of us out there, in every walk of life. Dylan was one, so are judges, governors, Cabinet members, bankers, police commissioners, schoolteachers...the list goes on." For some reason, this admission shocked me, and he saw the look in my eyes as I blurted out, "Really, Andy? You never struck me as the religious type."

He slurped the last drop in the glass, nodded to the bartender, and smiled: "I guess I deserved that, too."

I apologized, but he waved it off. "David, don't worry about it. You're right. I never gave a damn about religion. But, when I was representing Ed Vance in this case, interviewing him at Angola over fried chicken and biscuits as big as dinner plates, I found a tranquility in him that I began to...I don't know...crave. One day, Ed asked me if it ever bothered me that a gift as precious and serene as the Gospel of Jesus Christ had been preached for more than two thousand years, but had left no tangible results in the way humans conducted themselves in the here and now. 'It's as if Christianity was some kind of eternal soap opera shown for one hour a week and largely ignored as a vital force,' he said to me. I'll never forget that, David." Andy gulped his drink and glanced at himself in the mirror just above my head; no matter how spiritually advanced he purported to be, he was as vain as he had been in Professor Hardwick's class.

"Jesus has become nothing more than the nebulous hero of some fairy tale called the Gospel which nobody takes seriously, but which is a convenient enough way to explain away the injustices of the world or the fact that not everything can be understood by our five senses. Ed's words really hit home for me, David. I mean, here is this guy in shackles and chains, being murdered slowly by a high-fat, high-cholesterol diet, and he's telling me that the Gospel is real and offers paradise on Earth as well as in eternity as long as you are willing to stake everything to usher it in. You have to be prepared to give up everything you own to share and share alike. Nobody is any better, nobody is over anybody else, make love and find solace in everyone, there is no marriage, there are no civil commitments or traditions, gay and straight and everything in between are all the same. In the end, there are only five simple rules which, if followed, would make the world an amazingly tranquil and fulfilling place, a place where love truly could become the 'bond of perfection,' as St. Paul put it. But, you have to be willing to risk everything, your freedom, your cultural suppositions, shit, even life itself, for the Gospel to be inscribed once and for all on their hearts...on *our* hearts."

For that split second, I liked Andy...no, I loved him...perhaps for the first time in all of the years I had known him, and I liked him because I felt his angst and vulnerability.

As if reading my mind, Andy chuckled. "I know you must think I'm full of shit, David, but meeting Hardwick and Judge Santa, getting involved in the Vance case and reading the *Revelation of Anakum*, it wasn't all just coincidence. There is no coincidence. Everything is occurring precisely as it must happen, and in an infinite universe of infinite possibilities, it's inevitable that everything that occurs happens intentionally; what's more, it will happen again, in exactly the same way, in some other existence. I think that's what Borges wrote somewhere." He finished his martini and wiped his lips with a paper napkin.

I think that's what Borges wrote somewhere. Those were the last words Andy Sear, the most unlikely of prophets, ever spoke to me. I spent the next five months correcting the proofs of what was soon to be the revised English translation of the *Revelation of Anakum*. The earlier edition, the one that Ed Vance probably had kept in his cell at Angola, was sloppy and full of errors, and the initial editors failed to understand that certain words which they left untranslated were not Guaraní at all, but Maltese or Arabic. Surely even my old friend Dr. Goma had not known that.

Every month I would put one revised chapter in a manila envelope, which I was instructed to sign across the flap and seal with red wax, and send it by courier to an address in Reston, and every month I would receive a personal check from some woman in New Orleans with the words "house cleaning" neatly written out on the memo line. I had Andy's phone number, but he had warned me before not to call it unless it was a matter of life and death, and even then to let the phone ring four times and hang up so that he would know to call me back. After my work was done, I waited to receive an "all clear" from Andy or someone, but months came and went by faster and faster. The memories began to fade. I realized that I was unemployed again. One Saturday, resenting Andy's ingratitude, I pulled the slip of paper out of my wallet and hesitatingly dialed his number, but I could not let it ring four times because it was out of service.

Sometime in April, my doorbell rang and two Mormon missionaries, both clad identically in black and white, stood before me. Elder Roscoe and Elder Lorenzo. I don't know why I found it funny that both of their names ended in the same vowel, but I smiled faintly. When I asked what I could do for them, they apologized genuinely for bothering me and said that they had found a package on the bottom step, where the newspaper boy used to throw the *Times-Picayune*, and they wanted to make sure that it did not get waylaid. I thanked them, and they asked if they could return to talk to me about Jesus. I nodded "sure, another time" as I stared at the yellow package and locked the door.

The paperback within the yellow package was crisp and stiff. It had the intoxicating smell of glue and ink. *The Revelation of Anakum: A Revised English Translation*. On the title page there was a handwritten inscription in a barely legible, shaky handwriting:

David,

Spread the word that love is the bond of perfection. And don't forget that the correction is bloodless; the struggle is internal, not physical, but it is no less violent.

Andrew Sear